LIEUTENANT GARY

The Army ordered him to rescue the woman. "But don't get us into a war with the Indians. You're on your own." Only one man in all Texas could help him.

GUTHRIE McCABE

He sold whiskey to the Indians—and guns. But he could talk Comanche, think, feel and kill like one. He could get in and out of their camps like a greased otter.

GARY HATED McCABE—
BUT HE HAD TO RIDE WITH HIM!

Bantam Books by Will Cook

THE DRIFTER
TWO RODE TOGETHER

ABOUT THE AUTHOR

WILL COOK's lifelong knowledge of the authentic lore of the Old West and his deep love of the outdoors help account for both the excitement and solidity of his Western novels. Born on January 28, 1922, in Richmond, Indiana, Mr. Cook ran away to join the cavalry in Texas at 16, falsifying his age. When he realized that the cavalry was becoming mechanized and horses were being eliminated from the service, he transferred into the air force. While serving in the South Pacific during World War II, his leg was almost shot off, but he managed to return to duty in Alaska before the war's end. He stayed on in Alaska for a time as a bush pilot. Upon returning to the mainland, Mr. Cook eventually headed West, where, among other occupations, he was a deep sea diver, salvage worker, Judo instructor and deputy sheriff in the rugged Lake Country of northern California. When he wanted to turn his energies toward writing a definitive book on the art of Judo, his wife, Thea, encouraged him to write Western fiction instead. By drawing on his own life experiences and his extensive historical research, Mr. Cook was able to bring the early West to life in 56 novels and approximately 100 short stories in a 12-year span. There are over 1 million copies of his Western novels published by Bantam, including *The Drifter* and *Two Rode Together*, which was the basis for a classic John Ford film. In July of 1964, while building a schooner in his backyard in which he and his wife planned to sail around the world, Mr. Cook suffered a fatal heart attack.

TWO RODE TOGETHER

by Will Cook

ORIGINALLY PUBLISHED UNDER THE TITLE
COMANCHE CAPTIVES

TWO RODE TOGETHER
A Bantam Book / Originally published under the title
COMANCHE CAPTIVES

New Bantam edition / July 1961
2nd printing .... July 1979

A serial version of this story appeared in the
SATURDAY EVENING POST

Library of Congress Catalog Card Number 60–5386

ISBN 0–553–13044–7

Published simultaneously in the United States and Canada

Bantam Books are published by Bantam Books, Inc. Its trade-
mark, consisting of the words "Bantam Books" and the por-
trayal of a bantam, is Registered in U.S. Patent and Trademark
Office and in other countries. Marca Registrada. Bantam
Books, Inc., 666 Fifth Avenue, New York, New York 10019.

PRINTED IN THE UNITED STATES OF AMERICA

TWO RODE TOGETHER

1

Since his election as sheriff to Oldham County, Texas, Guthrie McCabe set his hour of rising for eight, and rarely varied it. Some people considered this lazy and swore that when election time came around they would throw their vote to a more industrious man. McCabe lived in the hotel, second floor, third door on the right, facing Tascosa's wind-brushed street. There was a small upper gallery just off his room and each morning he would stand there for a time, looking at his town, his adobe-mud town with its eternal dust and eternal wind to shift it about, and a near constant sun to keep everything beneath it roasted.

Beyond, southward, stretched Texas with its bigness and rivers, and the Llano Estacado, the Staked Plains, flat, lifeless scar of land with moaning winds and scant water; a place where a man could lose himself, or find himself, if that was his purpose. This was Guthrie McCabe's country. His because he wore a badge and ruled it with his rules.

After his look came a careful shave, the knotting of his tie, the buckling on of his big pistol. And finally his badge, his authority for all to see. McCabe was a big man, even for Texas, who liked her sons tall and hard. Without his boots he stood six-foot-one. With them he was much taller for he was just vain enough to wear the two inch Mexican "spikes," undercut so much that he seemed to walk a-teeter on his insteps. His face was like a cocoa bean, a brown that went deeper than a surface tan. The eternal wind had eroded lines around his eyes which had nothing to do with his thirty-four years; there was no mark of worry or care on his face, save for an unusual gravity of expression. He had brown hair, and a full mustache, curled at the ends. Sideburns came to the hinges of his jaw and were trimmed daily to blade sharpness.

Although his job demanded only occasional riding, Guthrie McCabe was never without his spurs, full Mexican rowels, four inches in diameter; they dragged with each step, scuffing floors, making a bell-like jangle that announced his approach.

He took his meals in the hotel dining room, at eight-thirty, and the Mexican waiter knew exactly what to bring, for Guthrie McCabe's habits were definitely established in Tascosa. He never hurried at the table, and afterward, he put a match to a short, Mexican cigar. While he took this brief pleasure, he saw a small cavalry patrol pace the length of the street, then pass on to dismount at the stable near the street's end.

The hotel clerk came through the dining room, gathered McCabe's dishes and took them into the kitchen. He dumped them a-clatter in the sink, then paused at McCabe's table on the way back.

"Wonder what the cavalry wants this time?" the clerk said.

McCabe lifted his glance briefly, then worked the cigar to the opposite corner of his mouth before speaking. "Go down the street and ask the lieutenant, and come back and tell me."

McCabe scraped back his chair, laid a quarter on the table, then walked out through the lobby.

A glittering sun bounced a-dazzle from the tawny street and turned the adobe walls of the buildings to gold. McCabe watched the cavalry detail farther down. The officer in charge detached himself and walked back toward the hotel, saber in hand to keep it from flogging his leg. He was a young man, twenty-six or seven, and already hardened by a tour of frontier duty. His hair was blond, ragged beneath his battered campaign hat, and the solitary first lieutenant's bars sewn into his shoulder boxes were faded and frayed by innumerable launderings.

When he stopped at the porch edge, he took off his hat and grinned. "What is it, McCabe? Ninety in the shade?" The lieutenant needed a shave and dust lay in the creases of his clothing. "Trade you jobs."

"Army pay is poor," McCabe said. "How's Fort Elliot?"

"Dull, hot, and dusty," the lieutenant said. He swiveled his head around and looked up and down the street. A few horses stood idle by the hitchrack in front of the saloon, and farther down, a freight wagon was making up for the run to Red River Springs. "You don't have it much better," the lieutenant said. He twisted his yellow neckerchief around and wiped sweat from his face. The dust in the cloth left muddy streaks from temple to neck.

"You want a bath?" McCabe asked.

The lieutenant's manner brightened. "At any price." Then he let his pleasure fade. "No. It wouldn't look right, Guthrie, me showing up shaved and bathed while my men stayed dirty." He put his hat back on and pulled the sweatband down to his eyebrows. "What kind of a mood you in this morning, Guthrie?"

McCabe shrugged. "Jim, does it really matter much?" He squinted at Jim Gary. "Did you ride all the way here to see me?"

"Partly," Jim Gary said. "Can I buy you a drink, Guthrie?

2

I've been thinking of a beer all the way in from Spindly Creek."

"Nothing in town but hot slop," McCabe said. "Not fit to drink."

"The men will appreciate it anyway," Gary said. He frogged his saber high, then stripped off his gauntlets. Sweat had soaked through the leather and darkened the backs of the fingers. "The colonel wants you to come to Fort Elliot, Guthrie." He did not look at McCabe when he said it, but after it was said, Gary raised his eyes to study him.

McCabe said, "Can't that man take no for an answer?"

"Doesn't seem like it, does it?" Gary smiled. "We'll leave tonight and travel while it's cooler."

"If I go." Then McCabe looked down the street at the waiting detail. "Well now," he said. "You brought some help, huh?"

"If you think I'll need it," Gary said. "Sorry, Guthrie, but the invitation is official."

McCabe remained thoughtfully silent for a moment, then laughed. "Gary, it's going to be a long ride for nothing, but I might as well go and get it over with for good."

"Thought you'd see it that way. You'll have supper with me? Good." He slapped McCabe across the stomach with his gloves, then walked down the street to his waiting troopers.

McCabe spent the day idling around town, and in the evening he went to the stable and saw that his horse was saddled, his gear properly stowed. Then he walked back to Tascosa's main street and found Gary in a small Mexican restaurant. When Gary saw McCabe, he pushed back a chair so McCabe could sit down.

"Too late for me to order something?"

"No," Gary said, and signaled the cook, who had a plate ready. The cook brought a plate of chili beans and tortillas, and McCabe began to eat.

Gary studied him for a moment, then said, "Are you going to turn the old man down again?"

"In person this time," McCabe said.

"Why?"

"Because this is army business. Let the army handle it."

"It's been my observation," Gary said, "that the Comanches, particularly Iron Hand, would rather do business with a civilian than a soldier. Every time he sees dirty-shirt blue he remembers a lot of his dead friends." He reached into his pocket for a key winder watch, glanced at it, then leaned back in his chair. "We'll leave in thirty minutes. That suit you?"

3

"I'm easily satisfied."

Gary frowned. "Are you, Guthrie?"

McCabe looked at him. "What's that supposed to mean?"

By rising, Gary ducked the question. He was standing on the sidewalk, enjoying his cigar when McCabe came out of the restaurant. O'Reilly was putting the detail together down the street, inspecting it, seeing that all flaws were corrected.

"Is the army going to put the Comanches on reservation?" McCabe asked.

Gary turned and looked at him. "No, I haven't heard anything about it. Why?"

"They ought to. Indians ruin a country. They make people nervous by just being around. The counties south of here could be full of ranches and farms if the Comanches were on reservation. Jim, people just won't believe that an Indian is peaceful, treaty or not."

"You figure it that way?"

"I figure what's best for Guthrie McCabe." He looked at O'Reilly and found him standing at the head of the waiting detail. One of the troopers had gone to the stable for McCabe's horse; he ducked under the hitchrail and stepped into the saddle.

Gary mounted: the cavalry detail formed a small group. Gary gave the hand signal that turned them and they left Tascosa, taking the road south, McCabe and Gary in the lead.

Twilight gave the plain a purple immensity and the grasses nodded to the day's last breeze. Even though the sun died, heat radiated from the ground as though some fire had been banked there, and the wind dwindled to a hot, feeble breath, just as though someone had shut a door, closing off the draft. The wind would stay down until the day's heat left the earth, then it would spring up again, bringing with it all those wild flavors of uninterrupted miles.

The column stopped every two hours, and dismounted on the hour to walk the horses. Canteens came out, gurgled, then popped when the corks were replaced; there was no other sound, and the slightest noise seemed magnified for a moment before it was lost in the vastness.

There was little talk until they reached Squaw Creek, then Lieutenant Gary, ordered a twenty minute stop-over, to refill the canteens and water the animals. Guthrie McCabe lit a cigar and squatted by the creek. The heat was dying off, leaving perspiration salty on his skin, leaving him unpleasantly gamy. Around him swirled the thick aroma of nitrogen and the sweetness of cut-plug chewing tobacco, and the strong skunk-odor of bodies unbathed for three weeks.

When the men were at ease and Gary was satisfied as to

4

their comfort, he came over to McCabe and hunkered down.

"You fuss too much," McCabe said.

Jim Gary grinned. "I'd argue that point with you."

"It's my opinion. But every man shoes a horse differently, Jim."

"True. You know, when I was at the Academy, a colonel gave us a lecture on leadership, and he never said a word. He just cut a ten-foot length of rope and laid it on the floor. Then he took the hind end and tried to push it. When that didn't work, he walked around to the other end and pulled it. That's the way I want to handle men, Guthrie."

"Up to now I've had no trouble making a man go."

Gary laughed. "You don't give a damn whether a man likes it or not, so what am I talking about? Let me have one of your good cigars."

"You ever try buying your own?" McCabe handed him one.

"Not on a lieutenant's pay. I've got two younger sisters to support."

"I didn't know that."

"Well, I don't talk much about it," Gary said. "My father was in the army too, you know. A sergeant-major in B Company." He paused to light his cigar. "Killed on the Rosebud. I was ten years old at the time. Cora and Alice were in pigtails."

McCabe said, "I had no idea you had it that tough."

"Not tough," Gary contradicted. "Just not easy, that's all. Relatives raised us, my mother's folks. On a farm in Iowa. They died six years ago in an accident. The horse balked at a railroad crossing and the Rock Island limited hit them. We sold the farm; it gave Cora and Alice enough money to buy a place in town and still leave a little in the bank. Since then I've been keeping twenty dollars for myself and sending sixty a month home." He chuckled. "Now you know why I don't buy nickel cigars."

"One of these days," Guthrie McCabe said, "they'll up and marry and you'll never hear from them again. Then you'll wish you'd kept some of that money for your own pocket."

"No, I wouldn't wish that. I never expected to get it back." He twisted his lower body, trying to find a more comfortable position. "You have to do for your kin. They'll get married one of these days and then I can quit sending them money, but it's nice to know that they never really wanted for anything, or had to take in washing to make a living."

"You have to look out for yourself."

"That's a philosophy you get from being alone," Gary said.

"Alone?" McCabe laughed. "Jim, I've got eleven brothers

and sisters—somewhere. You didn't know that, did you? Well, I never talk about it. They don't know I'm alive and I don't know where they are." He fingered the ash off the end of his cigar. "The old man was all prod and talk. When we moved across the country in '64, things got tough, mouths became hard to feed. He started kicking the boys out a hundred miles from St. Joseph. The oldest was the first to go. Ma did a lot of crying over him, but a thousand miles and six sons later, she got used to it. He put me out of the wagon not more than twenty miles from here. Ma never even looked around when they pulled away. There was a place on the prairie; I could see it, so I went there. A man takes what's easiest, Jim, so I took Anson Miles's cussedness for ten years. You took the army."

Jim Gary shook his head. "There's a difference, Guthrie. I like the army. It's what I want. What do you want?"

The tall Texan thought for a moment, then said, "I want to walk down the main street of any town in Texas and have people smile and tip their hats to me." Gary raised his head and peered through the gloom at this man, cocked his ears to the voice, for he had never heard it before, nor suspected the drive behind this man's bland manner. "And when I speak I want other men to stop talking and listen to what I have to say, and when I'm through talking, I want them to jump and do what I want done." He looked at Jim Gary. "Maybe that's too blunt for you, or too big for you to understand."

Jim Gary searched his mind for an answer, and found none. "Time to get going," he said and stood up, brushing dust off the seat of his pants.

Gary signaled for the men to mount up and they moved in the face of the southwest breeze that was freshening. At midnight the cavalry stopped for an hour's rest, and the troopers immediately stretched out for a quick nap. Jim Gary came in off the temporary line and sagged wearily beside McCabe. He folded his gauntlets and put them on top of his hat, making a pillow of the whole thing.

"How long has it been," Gary asked, "since you've been out to Anson Miles's place?"

"A year. Maybe longer."

"His wife asked about you the last time I stopped there." He looked at McCabe. "It's none of my business. Sorry."

"Hate to see a man break one of his own rules," McCabe said, "and you've always been hell on minding your own business. Now me, I mind everybody's business. I've lived twenty-three years in this part of the country. Know it like a book, every whoop and hollow from here to the Rio Pecos. Know most of the Indians too, over half of them by sight. I don't think there's a white captive taken, killed off, traded, died, or married that I don't know about. Jim, I'm personally acquainted with every rancher, every badman, cow thief, gunslinger, preacher, widow, and virgin in this part of Texas, although I ought to add that I've reduced the number of the last considerably. To my mind there isn't a shod horse within eighty miles that I can't identify by track, tell you who owns him, just how much he paid, what mare dropped him, or what stud sired him. I call the cattle by name and the wind sings my song. Twenty-three years I've stood the damned heat and the dust and a lot of trouble to know all these things, so when anyone wants anything from me, including your colonel, he has to pay for it. If that sounds tough, then just remember that every man has something to sell, and I never give anything away for free."

"How high is your price?"

"A thousand dollars for every one I bring back," McCabe said. "Then, and only then will I take the job."

Jim Gary thought about this, then said, "The Comanches and Kiowas have had nearly twenty-five years of war in which to take women and children. Since they're the only Indians who keep slaves, it's natural to think that a lot of them would still be alive. Guthrie, you ought to see the camp outside the post. I'll bet there's thirty families there, all hollering for the army to bring back the lost, strayed or stolen. Your price is a little high, seems to me."

"It's the value I place on my services," McCabe said. "You're free to get someone else to go into Comanche country, Jim."

"There isn't anybody who knows what you know."

"Then don't quibble about the price. Look, Jim, I got kicked off a wagon and landed here with my ass out of my pants and a snotty nose. Anson Miles gave me a handout and that's the way it's been, one handout after another, until I got smart and began listening and learning and nosing around. Folks began to learn that if you wanted to know a thing, ask the McCabe kid. I've got that kind of a mind, Jim. Pick things up easy and hang on to what I learn."

Sergeant O'Reilly came around and Jim Gary got to his feet. Corporal Bushkin was having the mounts brought in from the picket line and the detail formed quickly. The talk between Gary and McCabe seemed ended, yet the silence was unsettled, like the quiet after an argument when both parties expect to resume it more feverishly.

2

Through the cool of night and the gauze grayness of early dawn they pushed south, while in the east a streak of light marked the horizon and then the first orange rays of the sun washed across the flats.

In the distance, a little over a mile, Anson Miles's house was plainly visible, a high, three-storied saltbox house with ridiculous gables and scrimshaw work, a thirteen-room monument to bad taste and misspent money, sitting alone and weathered on a barren plain. This was a landmark and it reared ugly and uncompromising against the line of horizon.

"A big house for one man and one woman," Gary said softly. "When I get his age, I want people around me."

"He's got hired hands," McCabe said. He looked sharply at Gary. "Do you think I owe him anything? I worked double for everything he gave me."

"Don't we all?" Gary said.

When they were several hundred yards away, a dog charged toward them, yapping and showing his teeth. He ran between the horses, causing two to crow-hop. One of the troopers took his carbine by the barrel and cracked the animal solidly across the rump as he dodged about; surprised and somewhat pained, the dog tucked its tail between its legs and scooted for the shelter of the house.

Anson Miles hobbled out as McCabe and the cavalry dismounted before the broad porch. Miles was a man in his early sixties, unshaven, foul of temper and manner now that he was permanently lamed. His wife came to the doorway, a much younger woman; she could easily have passed for his daughter. She shielded the glare of the sun from her eyes with a flattened hand.

"Which of you buggers hit my dog?" Miles wanted to know. He looked at each of the troopers, sending his accusing scowl along the line. He was a small man, with a small man's tendency toward belligerence; he acted as though he were being put upon continually. Miles's face was not unhandsome, yet he wore the pinched expression so common among people who nurse dissatisfaction with living.

"Could we have some water?" Jim Gary asked, keeping his voice pleasant. He looked past Miles, then swept off his hat. "The heat bothering you, Mrs. Miles?"

"I pay it no mind. It vexes Anson though."

"I'll live through it," Miles snapped. He flung an arm toward the creek near the barns. "It's nigh dry now. You might as well finish it."

"You'll get rain in another month," Gary said. He dismounted and motioned for O'Reilly to take the detail on.

"You said that the last time you was here," Miles said. Then he looked at McCabe. "I don't see much of you anymore." The cavalry was near the big barn, and Miles heard the barn door open. "Damn them soldiers! If they're in my feed bin again——" He stomped off the porch and darted around the house.

Gary slapped his gloves against his thigh and said, "I'd better look into this. Can I take care of your horse, Guthrie?"

"Thank you," McCabe said. As soon as Gary left, he stepped out of the bake-oven heat and into the shade of the porch. When he looked at Carrie Miles, he let his glance soften. She was a shapely woman in her late twenties. Her hair was dark and long and she liked to wear combs in it to bind it tightly, holding it away from her neck.

"I'd like to ask you in," she said, "but you know how Anson feels about you."

"It's all right."

"No, it's not all right." She paused a moment. "I don't get to see anyone out here."

McCabe spoke softly. "Then I should stop by more often."

This pleased her; a flush came into her cheeks. She patted her hair, then smoothed her plain dress. "He doesn't take me to town anymore. I guess he thinks I'd run away if he did."

"Find a man. Then you won't have to wait. A man would answer for you, Carrie." He saw Gary approaching and moved to the edge of the porch.

"I'm ready," Gary said.

"All right. In a minute." McCabe waited and finally Gary walked away again. When he was out of earshot, McCabe said, "I expect Anson goes into town on Saturday and comes back the next Monday?"

"Yes, but only once a month. It'll be three weeks now before he goes again."

McCabe did not look at her, but off in the distance. "Be something to look forward to, won't it? Likely my stay at Fort Elliot won't be long. I ought to be passing through here about then."

Gary was already mounted and shooting glances toward the porch; McCabe walked across the interval to the barn and stepped into the saddle. Miles said nothing and after thanking him again for the water, Gary turned out, heading the detail.

9

Fort Elliot lay to the east, a five hour ride, and Gary took care not to march too rapidly in the heat. They raised the fort before noon and O'Reilly dismissed the detail and tended the horses while McCabe went to headquarters with Jim Gary. There was not much activity on the post; the heat was oppressive and only the detail men who had duty moved about. McCabe was surprised at the number of civilians. They clustered about the sutler's place, men, women, some children; they seemed to be waiting for time to pass.

Gary took McCabe's arm and ushered him into the front office. An orderly saluted, then knocked on Colonel Frazer's door. There was a murmur of talk, then the orderly stepped back so they could enter.

McKay Frazer was a man grown old in the service. His hair was shot with gray and the arid manner of his living seemed to have shrunk him; his arms were thin and flesh hung in wrinkled folds beneath his chin. He wore a full mustache, the ends upsweeping grandly. Frazer's face was like sun-baked clay, myriad cracks that ran into each other and recrossed silently. His nose was an arch of bone, curving, ending in wide nostrils. His eyes were matching agates sheltered in deep sockets and screened by gray bushy eyebrows.

"Sit down, McCabe." He opened a box of cigars and offered one to each of them. "I'll try to make the long ride worthwhile." Frazer struck a match on the underside of his desk, then leaned forward so both men could take a light. "Did you see the civilian camp near the south gate?"

"No," McCabe said. "But there were quite a few on the post."

"They come in for supplies," Colonel Frazer said. "It's good business for the sutler, but hell on the commanding officer." He tipped back his chair. "Most of those people have been out here before, McCabe. Some as far back as twenty years ago. And they all lost a part of their families to the raiding Comanches. Now that there's peace they want to find the lost ones. They think it's an army job to return them."

"It is," McCabe said.

McKay Frazer frowned. "We both know that it's a job the army can't do. Not without trouble, and Washington won't stand for that. Peace came too dear."

"Send the civilians home then."

"No. They write letters and congressmen put pressure on the generals and it all comes back to me." Frazer sighed. "We'll solve it right here, McCabe. At Fort Elliot. I need you, and I'll pay you chief scout's wages."

McCabe glanced at Gary, who was studying the stitching

10

in his gloves, then he looked at Frazer and smiled. "My price was a little higher, Colonel."

"All right. Perhaps I can stretch the point a little."

"About a thousand dollars a head for every captive I return?"

Blood mounted angrily in Frazer's face; it was a moment before he could speak. "McCabe, this is not a business venture, but a Christian service." He put his cigar into a glass dish. "Shall we consider your remark a bad joke, McCabe?"

"Consider it my lowest offer," McCabe said flatly. He leaned forward. "Colonel, if you take troops south into Comanche country they'll think it's a violation of the treaty and you'll have war again. You need a civilian, one who knows them and can come and go without losing his hair. Now I set the price. You either meet it or not."

"The general would never allow me to spend that kind of money and you know it!"

"You pay me chief scout's wages then. I'll make up the balance from the civilians." He studied Frazer's anger, then laughed. "Colonel, don't let your temper get the best of you now."

Frazer got up and turned his back to McCabe as though he could no longer bear to look at him; he stared out the window at the shimmering parade ground. "It's a pity," he said, "that we are forced to do business with those who disgust us the most. These civilians know that Lieutenant Gary went to fetch a man; rumor got out and spread rapidly because it was something they wanted to believe, that you were a messiah come to deliver them." He spun around on his heel and stared at McCabe. "That too is a pity, that they'd put trust in a man like——" He closed his mouth with a snap. "We'll keep this impersonal. Better that way. And as soon as the job is done, I can throw you off the post with a clear conscience." He waved his hand. "Find him suitable quarters, Gary. And I don't mean in the guardhouse, although the thought delights me."

"A pleasure to do business with you," McCabe said, and followed Gary outside.

Gary said, "I thought you'd back down the last minute."

"I don't back down," McCabe said as they crossed the parade toward the officers' picket quarters. "You share the colonel's opinion?"

"Maybe. I've never had a chance to make a lot of money. So I can't say what I'd do."

The quarters were no worse, no better than any occupied by the junior officers on the post. A small room, one cot, two chairs, a chest of drawers, a desk, and a closet, nothing

11

more. McCabe looked around, then shrugged. "It's not the Palace Hotel in Denver, is it?"

"No. I'll have an orderly bring your blankets later. Do you want to see the civilian camp?"

"Why not?" McCabe said. He smiled. "Jim, tears won't shake my price."

"Tears?" He looked questioningly at him. "Guthrie, you've got it all wrong. They stopped crying a long time ago."

"Then why all the fuss to get their kin back? Hell, we both know that after three or four years, a captive is free to leave when he wants to. Don't these people know that?"

Gary nodded. "They know it, but I guess they still had to come back. Some people have to do the right thing, no matter what it costs them." He stepped onto the porch and walked toward the side gate, McCabe following him. "But I'd keep out of Colonel Frazer's way, if I were you. He's got five months to go before retirement, and if it weren't for preserving a good record, he'd throw the book at you."

"He wants a record, and I want money," McCabe said. "Show me the difference, Jim."

"Can't, because I want a few things myself. Not big things though. I guess you'd say that I think small; it's a failing of mine."

The guard at the water gate brought his carbine to present arms, then passed Gary and McCabe through. The civilian camp was backed up to the creek, occupying the entire cottonwood grove. Tents, lean-to shelters, wagons, all crowded together in disorder as though someone had called a halt to all movement and wherever they were at the time, they stayed.

"How long have they been here?" McCabe asked.

"Some since the last rain, nearly four months ago."

"They ought to go home," McCabe said. "The country was too tough for them before, and it hasn't changed much." He stopped as a man walked toward them.

"That's Wringle. He's something of a leader here," Gary said. "Hello there, Mr. Wringle."

"Is this the man we've waited for?" Wringle had a deep voice and words rumbled in his chest. His clothes were blue overalls and a brown shirt, frayed at the collar and elbows.

"This is Guthrie McCabe," Jim Gary said. "He may take you into the country south of here."

"What's this?" McCabe asked. "Man, I go alone or not at all."

"Well, I was supposed to explain that to you, Guthrie. I guess it slipped my mind. The colonel wants the grove cleared

12

out, so he thought it would be all right if they all went south with you. There's good land there and——"

McCabe took Gary by the arm and pulled him around to face him. "You knew this in Tascosa?"

"Like I said, it slipped my mind."

"It did like hell! Jim, if I'd have known this, I wouldn't have ridden with you."

"I know it. So I kept quiet about it." He made an appeal with his hands. "Is this asking too much? It'll save you considerable riding back and forth. Last month I took a patrol south. There's a spring and timber about forty miles from here. They could camp there while you did your looking."

McCabe frowned. "I'll have to think about this." He turned his head and looked at the camp as though studying it, gauging the poverty of it, or its wealth.

"We've come a long way," Wringle said, "and suffered years of disappointment to be turned down now on a man's whim."

"Friend, my whim decides whether Iron Hand's Comanches give up their prisoners or not," McCabe said.

"That's right, Mr. Wringle," Gary said. "Mr. McCabe can do business with Iron Hand when no one else can."

Wringle thought about this for a moment, then said, "Seems funny to me that one man could be so friendly with——"

"I used to sell whisky to him," McCabe said and watched the disapproval rise in Wringle's eyes. "You don't like that, Wringle?"

Wringle looked at Gary. "It ain't for me to sit in judgment of a man. Not when getting my boy back depends on him. You see, I lost my boy about twelve years ago. On the way to El Paso. The heart sort of goes out of a man when that happens." He shrugged his beefy shoulders. "All I want is my boy back. Don't care how it's done or who does it."

"I didn't think you did," McCabe said. "Tell your people I'll drop over later tonight. We'll talk about this."

Wringle frowned, then asked. "What's there to talk about? You either go or you don't."

"You don't have the notion that I'll go for nothing, do you?" He took Gary by the arm. "Let's go get a drink." Gary opened his mouth to say something, then thought better of it and followed McCabe back to the water gate. As they stepped inside, Gary looked back at the civilian camp.

"What did you tell him that lie for? About selling whisky to the Indians?"

13

"To prove that a man will sleep with the devil if it gets him what he wants. The sutler's whisky any good?"

"No, but I've got a decent bottle in my chest of drawers," Gary said.

"It'd better be full," McCabe said and cut across the parade.

In his room, Gary set up the glasses and poured.

"Are you going to take them south?"

McCabe shrugged. "After tonight I'll know." He drank his whisky and set the glass down. "After tonight I'll know if they have any money or not."

"Comes back to that, does it?" Gary sat down on the edge of his bunk. "You want a lot of money. Can a man ask why?"

For a moment it seemed that McCabe was not going to answer. Then he said, "Anson Miles owes nine years in back taxes on his place. I want to buy it."

"That eyesore?"

"All in the point of view," McCabe said.

Gary said, "I don't think it'll pay you back for all the years you lived under Anson's foot."

"Might be that way. It just might be."

"Then it was for nothing."

"No," McCabe said. "I'll put a match to the place and have the biggest bonfire in Texas." He raised his glass. "This is good whisky, Jim. It sort of evens it out for the cigars."

"That's a funny thing to say."

"Is it? I guess I'm naturally suspicious of any man who doesn't indulge himself in something," McCabe said. "But now I won't have to be, will I?" He chuckled. "What's the frown for, Jim?"

"Just trying to figure out how much in you is good and how much is bad. Right now it seems important that I know," Gary said.

"When you find that out about any man," Guthrie McCabe said, "then tell me because it wouldn't be fair just to have one smart man in the world."

3

The invitation to have supper with Colonel Frazer took Jim Gary completely by surprise; he barely had time to shave and change into a clean uniform before it was time to dine. In the back of Gary's mind always lay the hope that someday he would advance to this rank and live in a big house with three enlisted servants, dwelling as graciously as one could under frontier conditions; this occurred to him as he was ushered into the colonel's parlor and handed a glass of sherry.

"Short notice, I know," Frazer said. "But I'm glad you could come, Gary."

"It was kind of you to invite me, sir."

"Have a chair. Try that leather one; I think you'll find it comfortable." Frazer sat down across from Gary. "Somehow a good sherry is made better by company." He put his glass aside. "I suppose McCabe is at the camp pinching purses."

"He told them he'd speak to them this evening, sir."

Frazer drummed his fingers for a moment. "I hate a man like McCabe, always after something, always something more than he has." He sighed heavily. "Well, in a few more months I'll be out of here, Gary. With luck, I'll retire a brigadier." He studied Jim Gary from beneath the thicket of his brows. "How long have you been in grade?"

"Nearly four years, sir."

"Do you know where you stand on the list?"

"Twelfth, I think."

Frazer nodded solemnly. "That'll mean another year at least, Gary. Seems a shame. You're a good officer with a lot of promise."

"That's very flattering, sir."

"It's the truth; that's why I said it; I rarely flatter a man just to be doing it. Care for some more wine? No? I think I'll have some. A good wine always adds something just before a meal. We have damned few graces on the frontier. You didn't know my wife, did you?"

"No, sir. It was never my pleasure."

"A good woman," Frazer said. "She took the heat and the discomfort for twenty-seven years, God bless her, and I never once heard her complain, although she had reason to." He smiled. "Is there a woman some place for you, Gary?"

"No, sir. The army's my life, sir."

15

"A lonely life without a woman, Gary. Better find one." He waved his hand. "There ought to be someone in the civilian camp, some pretty girl no one has noticed."

"I'll have to look, sir."

"You do that. Consider it an order." Frazer drank some of the wine. "Ticklish business this trying to locate lost relatives. As a final assignment to cap off a clean career, I can think of some more preferential. And this man, McCabe, will make trouble. A thousand dollars a head!" Frazer snorted briefly. "If I had more time, I'd send him packing and find another man. You've known him for some time, Gary?"

"Yes, a few years."

"Strange," Frazer said. "I mean, you and McCabe being friends. One man by training and instinct a gentleman, a man of honor, and the other a profiteer of the lowest sort, a man obviously with neither honor nor conscience." He shook his head. "There's an old saying about strange bedfellows, Gary. Most apt in this case."

"McCabe has always been honest with me, sir."

"Has he? Wait until he wants something from you. No, I must tolerate him, but I'll never trust him. That's why I'm placing you on detached duty, Gary. You'll go into the Comanche stronghold with him, out of uniform, of course." Frazer finished the wine and pushed bottle and glass aside. "Gary, I'll be frank with you. The general has given me a difficult assignment and if I want to go out a brigadier, I'll have to complete it without trouble. Do you think I'll enjoy a decent night's sleep until McCabe leaves my province? I'm sure I won't. But it will ease my mind if I know that you're there, to take over in the event he gets out of hand. Gary, I can pull some weight in Washington, and I can have you set up on the promotional list. This isn't a promise, mind you, but a strong possibility exists that you'd make captain within three months. Six on the outside." He leaned back and folded his hands. "I'm sorry to rush you like this, but there isn't much time. I'll need an answer tonight."

"Just what is it you want me to do, sir?"

"Keep McCabe from exploiting those people."

"How can I do that, sir? He's a strong man who does what he wants. When he was elected sheriff, the county wasn't fit to live in, with rustlers getting fat and toughs running the town. McCabe cleaned them out in three months; he's that kind."

"You're a resourceful young man, Gary. Think of a way. I'll give McCabe chief scout's pay, but not a cent more. The job will be done at my price, Gary, and that's final."

"Colonel, I thought you agreed———"

"With a rogue like McCabe?" Frazer laughed, and got up from his chair. "I believe dinner is served, Gary. Come along, and don't let your conscience trouble you where a man like McCabe is concerned." He took Jim Gary by the arm. "You've got a career to think of. A captaincy now will mean a majority before you're forty. What matters when you think of that?"

"I guess it doesn't matter," Gary said and sat down at the table, his manner grave and troubled. The soup was excellent, yet he ate mechanically, thinking about the things McCabe had said to him, about all men wanting something, wanting it bad enough to push all else aside to get it. And in that moment, Gary understood why he had tolerated the man; they were not dissimilar at all, except in method, and there McCabe was perhaps the more honest for he never hid his desires, even from himself.

Later, Gary left the colonel's quarters and walked across the dark parade to the water gate. He stood there for a time, watching the fires from the civilian camp, then on impulse, he walked over to the creek, stopping at the first fire he came to.

A woman was sitting there, shelling peas into a loop of cloth suspended between her knees. She looked up as Gary stopped, then said, "The men are gone. There's a meeting at Wringle's fire."

"I know about that," Gary said. He started to turn, to move on, then decided not to and stood there, watching the peas drop into her lap.

"There's some coffee left if you want some. The cups are in that chest over there." She pointed and Gary helped himself, conscious of her inspection. He placed her age as in the early twenties, but he wasn't sure about this for hard work and sun had darkened her skin and brought small wrinkles to the corners of her eyes.

"Your husband at the meeting?" he asked.

"My father and brother," she said. "Sit down if you want. I'm Jane Donovan." She squinted at his shoulder boxes; the fire did not give off much light. "You're an officer?"

"Lieutenant Gary. I'll be going with you, if McCabe goes."

"A lot depends on this man, doesn't it?"

"He knows the country, and Iron Hand. Not many white men does he call friend." He sat down on the wooden box and cradled the tin cup between his hands. He could see her face better now, oval, framed in dark hair. She had a long,

17

straight nose, and nice eyes, appraising, frank; he did not resent her open study of him, nor was he made nervous by it.

"You brought this man to us, didn't you? McCabe, I mean."

"Yes," Gary said.

"Then we're in your debt," Jane Donovan said. She put down the pan of peas and poured some coffee for herself. "It's my brother we seek. He was two when we lost him, nearly ten years ago. If he'd been killed instead of taken, I guess we could have accepted it. But it was my job to care for him, and when the Indians came I ran and hid."

"How old were you? Ten?"

"Eleven," she said. "I shouldn't have run. It's not a nice thing to live with, to know that it's your fault, a thing like this happening."

"And if you hadn't run," Gary said, "you'd be some buck's wife now, with a couple of half-breed kids."

"That would still have been better than this," Jane Donovan said.

"You don't know," Gary told her. "I've been in the villages and I've seen captives, dozens of them. The women would rather be dead than go back. Do you know what it would be like, pointed to, talked about, singled out, blamed for something you could not help?" He shook his head. "Be glad you ran and hid."

He turned his head as two men came out of the gloom and stepped up to the fire. Both were tall, bearded, and the older of the two stared at Jim Gary.

"You from the army? I don't want soldiers around here."

"This is Lieutenant Gary, Pa," Jane Donovan said. "My pa, Sean Donovan. And my brother, Liam."

Gary acknowledged the introductions, and before he could say anything else, Sean Donovan spoke. "This fella, McCabe's going to take us South. Leave day after tomorrow."

"Lieutenant Gary is going also," Jane said.

Her father and brother looked intently at him. "Was my understanding," Sean Donovan said, "that the army couldn't go into Comanche territory without stirring up a ruckus."

"I won't be in uniform," Gary said. He stood up. "Perhaps I'd better say good-night."

"No need to," Donovan said. "I didn't mean to sound unfriendly, but with a single woman——" He let the rest drop and wiped a hand across his mouth. "Sit down, unless you're in a hurry."

"It's a good feeling the way folks will help a man when he's got troubles." Donovan shook his head sadly. "A man's dreams and hopes are pretty fragile, Gary; they get smashed all-fired easy. We sold out in Iowa ten years ago and bought land here. After the lad was taken, we never went on. Never saw that land again. Had to sell it. Had to buy again in Iowa too. That's enough right there to break a man, Gary. And on top of it he's got to grieve." He reached out and put his hand on Jane's head. "I've been telling her every day that it wasn't really her fault, but I guess that don't do any good when you feel different inside. Hate to see her go on like this, doing penance this way."

Gary watched her carefully, observing the sudden tightening of her lips, the tautness, of her cheeks. Suddenly she pulled from beneath her father's hand and walked rapidly to the nearby trees; she stood there, her back to them.

Sean Donovan's expression was one of hurt. "Wish she wouldn't do that. Running away from a thing don't solve it."

"You went back to Iowa," Gary said softly.

"That's different," Donovan said.

"I suppose it is," Gary said, getting up again. He thought about going over to the trees and speaking to Jane Donovan, then decided not to. Cutting away from the fire, he walked toward the wagon park, stopping at another camp.

For nearly two hours he moved about, listening to the talk, hearing the same thing over and over again, about how much they had lost and why they had turned back instead of going on. He was touched by their talk, and irritated at the same time, for they were all defeated a long time ago, and had lived with it for years; there wasn't a teaspoon of hope in the lot of them, just excuses and reasons that sounded good to no one but themselves.

Finally he left the camp and went back to the post, going to Guthrie McCabe's room. The tall Texan was stretched out on his bed, patiently cleaning the grit from the bore of his pistol. He turned his head when Gary knocked, then motioned toward the chair.

"Been out to the grove, huh?"

"Yes," Gary said. "Donovan thinks you're the patron saint. A lot of them think that way." Gary dropped his hat to the floor and crossed his legs. "I wonder if they'd feel the same way if they knew you'd put a price tag on the whole deal. How come you didn't say anything about that, Guthrie?"

"You ever trade horses?"

"Sure."

"Then you ought to know that price is the last thing you talk about." He swung his feet to the floor and reassembled his revolver, then loaded it and slipped it into his holster, which hung on a wall peg. "Jim, after I look around a bit, and turn up someone, then I'll talk about price." He looked squarely at Jim Gary. "The old man sent you along to keep tabs on me?"

"He didn't say that exactly."

Guthrie McCabe laughed. "Don't play poker, Jim. You're a poor liar." He took out some sack tobacco and rolled a cigarette, then passed the makings over to Jim Gary. "I wish you wouldn't be such a do-gooder. It makes me nervous." He accepted a light, then leaned back, his shoulders against the wall, both hands hooked around an upraised knee. "What did you think of the pack living at the grove, Jim?"

"They're good people."

"They're rubbish," McCabe said flatly. "Cowards, quitters, failures. Something tough happens to them and they fold in the middle and run back home where it's safe."

"A pretty harsh judgment for such short notice," Gary said. "You could be wrong."

"I'm right, and you know it."

"Sure," Gary said. "You're right, but I'll be damned if I want to talk about it." He sounded angry. "I can look at the town drunk without sermonizing. Be a good idea if you did the same. What these people are is no concern of yours. How can you live among people when you don't respect them, or even like them?"

"Because they don't matter to me, that's how. The trouble with you, Jim, is that you try to do everyone a favor. One of these days, when the cards are down and the bets are made, you'll find out that the only one worth looking after is yourself. To hell with the other guy."

"McCabe, you're honest about it, I'll say that much." Gary took a final pull on his cigarette, then got up to throw it out the door.

"If you and I were in a tough spot together and it was run or die, I wouldn't hang back to save you. Not if it meant my own neck, I wouldn't."

"I'd try to save you."

"And I'd call you a damn fool for it."

"And I wouldn't believe you," Jim Gary said. "Guthrie, there must be two hundred people in the grove. For every four, there's a relative lost. How many do you think you can bring back?"

McCabe shrugged.

"Ten?"

"Maybe ten." He looked intently at Gary. "What do you want me to do, go out there and tell them that their sisters and daughters are squaws now with Comanche kids? Or that their sons and brothers are Comanche warriors who've raided and killed? Go on, you're the do-gooder. You go out there and tell them. They wouldn't believe it, not after farming a broken down section and saving their money to come back and look. Jim, it's a goddamn shame that people care so much. It would be a lot better for everyone if they cared less, and stayed home."

"You're working yourself up to a boil," Gary said, smiling. "I thought you didn't give a damn."

"I don't. If I did, I'd go back to Tascosa and sit with my feet on the desk. That damned deputy of mine probably has everything screwed up by now." He got up and walked to the door to stand. Someone came across the parade ground, and onto the porch. Gary caught a glimpse of skirts, then recognized Jane Donovan's voice when she spoke.

"Mr. McCabe?"

"Yes."

She looked into the room and saw Gary; he stood quickly, then came to the door. "Won't you come in?" he asked.

"No," she said. From a pocket in her apron she produced a tintype. "This isn't a very good picture, Mr. McCabe, and he was very young when it was taken, but it's all I have." She handed it to him. "I've been saving it, thinking it might help, but it's been ten years, and I don't suppose he would even speak English. He could only say a few words and——"

Jim Gary took her arm. "Perhaps I'd better walk you back to the grove."

"No, it's kind of you to offer, but I'll be all right." She turned then and hurried across the parade ground, and Guthrie McCabe watched her for a moment. When he turned back into the room he kicked the chest of drawers solidly.

Jim Gary said, "Kind of gets you, doesn't it? I mean, hanging onto so thin a hope all these years."

"Damn fools! They're all blind fools who can't understand that there isn't any hope." He tossed the picture on the bed, not looking at it. "I don't know what they're thinking, Jim. Probably that all I'll have to do is ride into Iron Hand's village and tell him to cough up the prisoners. My God, there must be twenty villages between here and the Rio Bravo, and if I do find someone, getting them back won't be easy. They just won't want to come back." He blew out a ragged breath. "I should have stayed in Tascosa."

"Maybe they'll see it after we camp south of here." Gary said. "Like you say, they're not hard to discourage. They went back home once. They might do it again."

"That's a thin hope. For twenty years Texans have been fighting the Comanches, hoping that someday there would be peace, and look at now, just a big mess to paw over and try to clean up. During the war there was an officer in charge of graves and burial, and I used to watch him go around after the battle, poking around the dead, going through their pockets, trying to identify them. His sleeves would get bloody and he'd get mud on his pants from kneeling, and I used to think then that it would be a hell of a lot better if they just buried them where they lay and forgot about it." He waved his arms. "Prisoners are traded and killed, and they die. It'll be like combing a dog for fleas, then trying to match up the parents with the children. And what about the years in between, Jim? All those years of living like an Indian? Thinking like an Indian? What do they do when they've been reunited? Take him back to Iowa or Indiana and let people stare at him because he eats with his fingers and farts at the table?" He slapped his hands together and sat down. "She brings me a picture. A goddamned picture taken when he was two years old, and hopes I can see the resemblance ten years later."

"Give it up then."

McCabe shook his head. "No, there's been too much giving up in that camp. Would you give it up, Jim?"

"I might because I'm not as tough as you. I'm the kind who cries at funerals."

"You'll never learn," McCabe said, "but then, with some people, it's just as well." He took out his watch and wound it. "I figured we could move out day after tomorrow; they can pack up and be ready to leave by tomorrow night." He put the watch back in his pocket.

Jim Gary picked up his hat and turned to the door. He paused there and said, "I'd have tried to tell them the truth, about how hopeless this all is. I'd try because I'm soft and I can feel sorry for them. Maybe you're doing them a favor, Guthrie. I mean, taking them back to where it all began and rubbing their noses in it for one final time. But I don't know. There ought to be an easier, a kinder way."

"There is. I could go back to Tascosa and leave them standing there." He sat down and took off his boots. "But there's no profit in that. For them, nor for me."

"Yes, I guess it boils down to that when all's said and done," Gary said. "I'll see you in the morning." He stepped out and walked rapidly down the walk toward his own quarters.

4

Gary had a letter to write to his sisters, then he changed out of his uniform, rolled what gear he would need, and carried this to the stable, along with his Winchester; the sergeant would see that his horse was saddled and everything stowed. He spent the remainder of the day in the grove, helping them get ready to move.

The farrier sergeant checked the stock, and Colonel Frazer detailed C Company to help them with their wagons and buggies and buckboards; one man drove a brewery wagon, the barrel racks removed so he could carry his possessions. At four in the afternoon, an orderly summoned Lieutenant Gary to the commanding officer's office. Guthrie McCabe was there, his chair tipped back against the wall. Frazer maintained an unfriendly silence until Gary closed the door.

"Take the other chair, Lieutenant." He rustled some papers, stuffed others in a dispatch case and handed it to Gary. "Here is the list of the missing, classified as to name, age when taken, and any physical description: hair, eyes, scars or marks. I want a thorough check made on anyone returned by Mr. McCabe."

"Yes, sir."

McCabe cleared his throat. "Which brings us to the trading goods. I thought I'd better mention it."

"What trade goods?" Frazer asked.

"Well, you don't expect them to give up a slave just because I ask them to, do you? I'll have to dicker a little, offer a trade. That's what I mean, trade goods."

"I could have sent anyone down there to trade!"

MccCabe said, "No trade goods, no prisoners. I suggest you load two wagons from the sutler's and take them along. This is just another little expense you're going to have to absorb, Colonel."

"I'm afraid he's right, sir," Gary said. "Shall I attend to it?"

"Yes," Frazer said. "But in a few minutes. That will be all, Mr. McCabe." He waited until the Texan went out, waited until the door closed and his footfalls had receded. "Take an inventory of the trade goods, Lieutenant, and keep accurate records. I don't want any of it to find its way into a Tascosa hardware store."

"Yes, sir."

"And there's one more thing. When someone has been re-

23

covered, to the best of your ability make certain that he is restored to the proper family. God knows I don't want someone to say later that we pawned off someone else's kin."

"That might be difficult to establish, sir."

"Difficult? Likely it will approach the impossible, but this whole thing is impossible, a political move to make the voters happy."

"Will that be all, sir?"

"Yes, and the best of luck. You'll be in a country rarely frequented by white men, and you'll be dealing with basically hostile forces, regardless of the treaty. On top of that you'll have to ride herd on a group of people who were never meant to live here, and you'll have to keep your eye on that thief with a sheriff's badge." Frazer spread his hands. "A captaincy comes hard, Gary, but I'm sure you'll earn it."

They shook hands briefly and Gary left the building. McCabe had gone back to the civilian camp so Gary had two wagons brought around to the rear of the sutler's place and began to select trade goods. He and three enlisted men loaded tools, blankets, bright cloth, beads, and two cases of worn-out military rifles. Gary was smart enough to select mainly the things a woman would want, for he knew that any buck who lost a slave would soon have to replace her with a wife, and that would take trinkets.

That evening the sound of music and laughter from the grove drew his attention; they had always been a solemn lot, and these sounds seemed out of place, alien to them. He left the post and walked to the creek, stopping at the Donovan wagon. Sean and Liam were sampling a jug while Jane sat on the food box and tapped her foot to the saw of violin, the wheeze of a small accordian.

"Not dancing?" Gary asked. He spoke to Sean Donovan, but his eyes sought the girl.

"The night's young," Donovan said and offered the jug. "Good to be leaving tomorrow. A man thinks of something for a long time, and then it comes to pass. You've been south. What's the country like?"

"Brush, hills. Water's scarce though. It'll populate now that the treaty's been signed. Land can lay for a long time, then someone who won't take no for an answer puts up a mud hut. The next thing you know, you got a town."

"I like that," Sean Donovan said. He tapped his son on the arm. "Let's go see where the fun is." He looked sternly at Jim Gary. "You keep good company with my girl, you hear?"

He stomped off, followed by his son, and when they were gone, Jane said, "He embarrasses me sometimes."

"No need to be," Gary said. "You don't mind my being here?"

"I'm glad you came," she said. "How long have you been in the army?"

"Nine years."

"Always out here?"

"Most of it."

"It must be lonely for you," she said.

"Yes, it is. But a man can't have everything. You see, I always wanted to be one of those men who forged ahead, found new horizons, but I've never had the courage alone. In the army, with men around, acting under orders, I can do those things without fear of failure. You might say that it's a combined strength. The army holds me up a little, and I like to think that I help hold it up. I wish you'd call me Jim."

"All right, if you like. Jim, I hope Mr. McCabe doesn't find my brother. I hope he's dead." She put her hand over her face and rubbed her eyes. "That was a terrible thing to say, but I've been thinking it a long time, so I decided to say it. It's not easy to say, and harder to keep thinking, but I'm not strong enough to live around him and have him know that I once deserted him when he was helpless."

"How many in the grove stuck by when the Indians attacked them? How many of them carry some secret loathing within them, Jane? How many do you think blame themselves for something that couldn't have been avoided?"

"I don't know, but if they all felt that way, it wouldn't help me." She got up and pushed the blackened coffeepot nearer the fire. Then she turned and looked squarely at him. "Jim, haven't you ever done anything you've been ashamed of? Haven't you ever wanted something you knew you had no right in having?"

"Sure, but I always got over it." From his pocket he took a cigar and bit off the end before taking a twig from the fire for his light. "Jane, suppose McCabe is lucky. Suppose he finds your brother. What then? I mean what will *you* do? Go back to Iowa?"

"I suppose. The farm is all we have, and pa spent the last ten years working his fingers to the bone paying for it." She got two cups out of the wooden locker and filled them with coffee. When she handed him his cup, she asked, "Is it important?"

"It would be to your brother. No one is really going to understand, or make allowances, not even here in Texas. It'll be much worse in Iowa."

"We never thought of that. You ought to talk to pa about

it." She sat down across from him and folded her hands in her lap. "You think we're wrong, coming here now that there's peace, don't you?"

"Yes, it was a mistake. With good intentions, but a mistake." He put his coffee aside. "After the battle, everyone wants the dead dug up and re-buried in the family plot. Nice sentiment, but a lot of trouble." He held up his hand when she opened her mouth to speak. "I know, your congressman promised you the army would co-operate. You did your crying once. Why do it again?"

"Because a thing isn't really done until it's finished," she said. "And until we know whether or not he's dead, it never will be finished."

"I understand," Gary said. "When I was a kid, I remember this preacher who went into the saloon every night to deliver his sermon against drink. And every night the boys threw him out, but he came back. Nothing could stop him, Jane. It was like he had a disease that only dying could cure." He finished his coffee and threw the grounds into the fire. "It's late and we have an early start in the morning. Good-night."

"Good-night," she said and watched him turn away.

He walked rapidly back to the post. As he passed through the water gate, he saw the courier arrive from Tascosa, mail pouches swollen. Perhaps there was something there from his sisters. He started toward headquarters to check the mail, then changed his mind and went to his room. If there was anything, Sergeant O'Reilly would pick it up.

His window was bright with lamplight and Gary opened the door. McCabe was on the bunk, reading; he put the book aside when Gary hung up his hat and pistol.

"I thought you'd be at the whoop-up," Gary said.

"Later," McCabe said. "There's some pretty fair-looking women in that camp." He patted his pockets for a cigar, found one and tipped the lamp toward him for a light. "I think we ought to have a little talk, Jim. About how it's going to be when we get into Comanche country." He thumped himself on the chest. "It's going to have to be my way, the way I say, and no arguments."

"I'm not going along to argue with you, Guthrie."

"Sure, sure, but you wear that soldier suit and the colonel gives you orders that I don't know anything about, and you're the kind who obeys orders." He looked steadily at Jim Gary. "Don't buck me, Jim. I won't stand for it."

"Then you play it straight," Gary said.

A smile built on McCabe's face, then he laughed. "I never charge more than the traffic will bear. That's why I get so

26

few complaints; I charge high, but a man gets his money's worth with McCabe." He got up from the bunk, the book still in hand. He glanced at the title, then tossed it on the chest.

He walked out and Jim Gary closed the door, sliding the bolt. The brooding, forbidding presence of Guthrie McCabe remained in the room, along with the aroma of his cigar, and this disturbed Jim Gary. In a sense, he was a little in awe of McCabe, and a little afraid, for the man seemed to reach out and squeeze, and afterward nothing was the same. There was a tremendous capacity for good in the man, and a latent talent for evil, and in Gary's mind, he could never separate the two.

He thought it strange that he could go through life with all good intentions, yet actually do very little that was materially good. Gary did his job with exactitude, and a certain amount of imagination, and when the job was finished, the edges were smooth, the details taken care of, but the mark remaining was never very lasting nor very deep. McCabe, on the other hand, cared little for good intentions and never entertained them, yet he left a wide path for a man to see, leaving in his wake somewhat of a mess, yet much came out of the things McCabe did. He was a builder, a rough, fast-working, self-centered builder, building for himself, working for himself, but the litter remaining was of great value to others.

Like McCabe and Iron Hand. It had been worth a man's life to travel south in the Comanche stronghold; some who tried never came back. Then McCabe hit on the idea of trading with the Comanches. They'd run down wild horses and McCabe would trade for them. Most men said it couldn't be done, but McCabe did it. He made a lot of money and broke a few local horse ranchers in the process, but Gary knew that McCabe had broken the trail that soon widened into a full peace negotiation with Iron Hand and the United States Army.

Settling down for the night, Jim Gary thought it strange that he could respect and resent a man at the same time. He was in awe of McCabe, and afraid of him. He admired and disliked him simultaneously.

"I've got to get over this," Gary told himself. "I've got to live with him for a while, so I've just got to get over this. Damn it, I'm my own man!"

27

5

A day south of Fort Elliot the land began to change, opening into gullies and rising to low ridges which made traveling more difficult with wagons. The first night they camped on the flats near Joe Sutro's place; this was the last white habitation for nearly eighty miles. Some of the travelers talked with Sutro and stared at his graveyard; a wife and nine children were buried there, all killed by Comanches during the raids to drive him away.

Gary had supper with Sutro; he liked the withered, rawhide-tough little man. The meal was simple; some sowbelly and beans and coffee strong enough to float a railroad spike; Sutro believed that coffee ought to be a meal unto itself.

"Surprised to see you with this bunch," Sutro said. "The army ain't often given to foolishness." He filled his mouth with beans and chewed rapidly; he had only four front teeth left. "How far you taking them?"

"Sand Creek," Gary said. "McCabe will go on alone from there."

"McCabe?" Sutro put his knife and fork down. "I didn't see him." He grunted once and began eating again. "Don't want McCabe around here. The sooner he moves on, the happier I'll be." He looked at Gary and grinned. "Nothin' personal, you understand, but I traded horses with him once. He talks too good and I persuade too easy. A month ago I lost some saddle stock. Couldn't afford to lose 'em either; a dozen horses represent a lot of money. Some of Iron Hand's bunch stole 'em, but I'll be damned if I'll risk my hair to go after 'em."

"You want McCabe to do it?"

"He could, if he would," Joe Sutro said. "Likely his price'll be high."

"I'll see what I can do," Gary promised. He finished what was left of his meal and walked over to where the wagons were parked. He asked at three different fires for McCabe, but no one knew where he was. Gary turned to the Donovan wagon, parked on the other side of camp.

Jane was alone, washing the pots left over from supper. "Have you seen McCabe?" Gary asked.

"No. Is there something wrong?"

"I just can't find him, that's all." He put his hands in his pockets and rocked back and forth on his heels. "Don't you

28

ever stop working? I mean, every time I come around, you're busy." He observed her a moment longer, then reached down and took the wet cloth from her and kicked the dish water into the fire. "Let's go for a walk, Jane."

Her eyes were round and surprised. "I can't."

"Sure you can." He took her arm and started her away from the steaming fire. "Out there the grass is talking and the night is black and the earth smells good. I want you to listen to the sounds and feel the darkness like a touch against your skin." He started to walk and she held back slightly, then gave in to his whim and walked beside him.

"Pa'll be roaring mad," she said.

"Let him be mad. I'll stand up to him if I have to." She seemed willing to let him have his way and he wondered whether or not he should relax his grip on her arm. He was reluctant to do so for her flesh was warm to his touch and he had almost forgotten how soft a woman was.

Fifty yards from the camp, Gary stopped.

"What's the matter?" she asked, then gasped when a man reared up from the knee-high grass.

Guthrie McCabe reholstered his pistol as they came toward him. He peered at Jim Gary. "You had three other directions to take to do your courting. Why pick this one?"

"An accident," Gary said. "I've been looking for you, Guthrie."

"So? If I'd wanted to be found, I wouldn't be out here."

"Just why are you out here, Mr. McCabe?" Jane asked. "I'd think you'd want to be around people. Do you like it alone?"

"McCabe's afraid to have friends," Gary said, half joking, then realized that he had inadvertently hit upon the truth, for McCabe stared at him rudely, then sat down.

"You're here. You might as well stay awhile. What did you want, Jim?"

Gary took off his coat so that Jane wouldn't have to sit on the ground. "I was talking with Joe Sutro. He's lost some horses."

"And he wants me to find them?" McCabe asked. "All right. Tell him I'll do it."

Gary did not try to hide his surprise. "No hitch, Guthrie?"

"Sure, but one Sutro wouldn't care about." He waved his hand to the south. "In three days I'll be leaving you, going into Iron Hand's country. But I've got to have a reason, one he'll buy. Joe Sutro's horses will do nicely. After I move around from village to village, looking for the horses, I'll have some idea of how rough this job is going to be, and who's left to bring back, or who'd be fool enough to come back."

He laughed. "I was figuring to run some stock south as soon as we camped permanently on Sand Creek. Sutro's saved me the trouble."

"One of these days you're going to do something for someone and get nothing for yourself, and then you'll die of a broken heart," Gary said.

"Don't hold your breath," McCabe said.

"Mr. McCabe, why is it that no one likes you?" Jane's question was so pointed, so blunt, that he could only look at her, his mouth slightly open.

Gary got up and took Jane by the arm. "Let's go on back. He wants to be alone."

"Hold on a minute." McCabe said. "Sit down. Here, Jim. have a cigar." He scratched a match on his belt buckle and in the brief glare, Gary studied him. Then McCabe whipped out the match and broke it before throwing it into the grass. "Miss Donovan, you just stuck your nose into my business, and I've never liked that from anyone. But since you asked, I'll tell you why no one likes me. It's because I don't want them to like me. Does that make sense to you?"

"No," she said, "because it goes against human nature. You care, Mr. McCabe. I know you care, and because you do, I wanted you to tell me why. You haven't, you know."

"Figure it out for yourself," McCabe said gruffly. "I never give free handouts, and that applies to advice. The world's full of mean people and sad stories and if a man caught all the kicks that were aimed his way, or listened to the stories, he'd be aching or crying all his life." The end of his cigar glowed redly as he drew on it. "A friend always wants something, and I've never felt obligated to give; no one gives to me."

"Perhaps they would if you'd let them," Jane said. She got up and handed Gary his coat. "I'd really better be getting back, Jim. If pa and Liam found out I'd gone off—well, I'd just better get back."

McCabe rose. "I'll walk back with you." He slung his coat over his shoulder and trailed them into the wagon park. As they approached the Donovan wagon, Gary saw Sean and Liam turn; there was a scowl on the old man's face.

"I'll have a word with you, Mr. Gary!" He waved his hand. "Get in the wagon, girl."

"Pa, don't say anything! Not anything at all!"

"You want me to be silent?" He looked at Gary. "I spoke to you before, but it seems you ignored my advice."

"We went for a walk," Gary said. "I don't know what you can make of it, but it seems that you're going to try."

30

Sean Donovan took off his coat and laid it to one side. Then he rolled up his sleeves carefully and hitched up his pants. Gary stood there while the promise of trouble collected a crowd, and he wondered what he should do, talk or fight. Talk would make him look weak and fighting would be something he'd have to answer for to the colonel.

"My daughter is a good girl, Gary, and a good girl has nothing but her good name, which is an easy thing to lose. Then she has nothing." He pushed his son aside. "Are you ready, Mr. Gary? Or do you wish to strike the first blow?"

Jane put her hands over her mouth, then whirled to McCabe. "Can't you stop him?"

"What for?" McCabe asked. "This is Gary's ball."

Sean Donovan was not a man who liked to wait for anyone; when Gary just stood there, he lost patience and charged, arms working like a two-bladed windmill. One fist caught Gary alongside the head, then he sidestepped the rest and danced back, fists cocked, but making no attempt to strike. Drawn up short, Donovan whirled and came in again, and this time Gary tried to smother the flurry of fists, getting a cut lip for his trouble, and a smarting patch on the cheekbone. He heard McCabe say, "You going to dance with him or fight him, Jim?"

He was right, Gary knew, and hit Sean Donovan, the blow a solid, axing drive that propelled him backward into the side of the wagon. In Gary's past was his share of barracks fighting, and he knew the dirty tricks, but he had a gentleman's reluctance to use them. But when Donovan came at him, spitting blood, Gary hooked into him, making him goggle-eyed.

Donovan was the heavier of the two, and he chose to wrestle, hugging Gary around the neck with a vise pressure, then flinging him over his hip to the ground. Donovan intended to fall with his weight on Gary's stomach, but the young officer had seen that once before and swayed to one side, leaving Donovan nothing but hard ground to break his fall. Raising his arm up and over, then locking the fingers, Gary forced Donovan's head back until he could raise a leg and hook the back of the knee behind his chin.

With a surge of power he brought Donovan's head down to the ground, then twisted and carried him over to land flat on his back. For several minutes the two men strained against each other, one to hold and the other to get free. Finally Donovan broke away and they both came to their feet, more cautious now, and more determined.

They drove together like two bulls in the first battle rush of spring, pawing, striking, cutting the earth with their boots,

31

then Gary caught Donovan behind the knee with a leg chop and hooked him to the ground. He hit him, a dry-twig-breaking sound, and strength ran out of the Irishman.

Quickly Gary got to his feet and stood over Sean Donovan as the man tried to rise, but he could not make it. Liam, his son, was at his side then.

"Pa! Get up, Pa!"

Donovan shook his head. "Can't. You finish this."

"I'll sure do that," Liam said and started to peel off his coat.

When it was halfway down his arms, Jim Gary struck him, kicking him clear off his feet. Liam Donovan rolled twice and ended on his face and knees. He struggled to his feet, ripping free of the coat; he threw it aside while Jane jumped between them.

"No! Liam, no!" She grabbed his arms while she made an appeal to Guthrie McCabe. "He can't fight two in a row! Help him!"

McCabe rolled his cigar from one corner of his mouth to the other before speaking. "I make it a point to keep out of another man's fights."

Liam shoved his sister aside and went after Gary, who was more tired than he realized. Sean Donovan had mauled him, wore him down, sapped his young first strength, and his speed. The two men rammed together, and it was Gary who gave ground this time, backing quickly to keep out of Liam's way.

He went down once, but was hardly conscious of it; the young Irishman was like the wind, coming in, bowling him over, then retreating to strike from a new direction. Gary put up his fight but it was not enough. Each second that passed seemed to take more out of him, and then he passed that point when he knew he could not possibly win this, just stay as long as he could stand.

Blood ran from Gary's nose, and his mouth, and a cut over the eye, but he seemed numb and when Liam hit him, he did not feel pain, only the jar of the fist landing. Twice more he fell and somehow got up and was promptly knocked down again.

Then someone fired a gun and he looked around to see who did it and saw Jane standing there with a cap and ball pistol in her hand, smoke dribbling from the barrel and cylinder. Liam was by the fire, shirt in shreds, blood and a surprised expression on his face.

"That's enough!" Jane said, tears in her eyes. She looked at the curious gathered around the fire. "Get out of here. Get!"

32

They moved when she flourished the pistol at them. Her father was standing by the wagon, and Liam joined him. McCabe remained back a few paces, then Jane put the pistol down and picked up the water bucket. Using her apron for a washcloth, she bathed Jim Gary's face.

Finally he sat up and drew up his knees, resting his head on them. He felt sick and angry, and sorry that he hadn't whipped Liam Donovan.

McCabe said, "You did all right while you lasted, Jim."

Gary remembered that he was there and swiveled his head around so he could look at him. A new anger came to him, the anger of being let down, deserted, like that time when he was a boy and a "friend" had agreed to help him beat up two other boys, then ran out and left Jim to do it alone. Gary said, "Guthrie, you'd better hope the day never comes when you have to ask me for anything."

"You'll turn me down?" He shrugged casually. "What does it matter anyway? I've never asked you for anything yet, have I?" He took a final pull on his cigar then shied it into the fire. "One way to look at this is that I did you a favor. You'd have had to fight both of them anyway; they're Irish. So a man might as well do it at one time and get it over with."

He turned then and walked back through the grass to his lonely camp. Gary stared after him a moment, then muttered, "God damn it, a man doesn't know what to believe, whether he was lying to cover himself, or telling the brutal truth." He looked at Jane Donovan then as though he expected to read the answer in her face.

She only helped him to his feet.

6

In the week it took to establish a permanent camp at Sand Creek, Lieutenant Jim Gary began to know and understand the people he was forced to live with. Timber was handy, and water, and they began to build cabins, to establish themselves with permanence; he was positive of this when Clyde Twokerry faced Hank Swilling with a rifle and ordered him off his "property."

Guthrie McCabe was gone, with a pack horse and trinkets; he intended to scout the Comanche villages to the south and east in search of Sutro's horses; Jim Gary was in charge of the camp.

Unlike the many movers he had known, these people stayed to themselves, bound by their clans, their families, their selfishness; there was very little "hand lending"; each shifted for himself.

The Twokerrys were from Minnesota, the old man, Clyde, his three boys, a talkative wife, and two young girls, the elder in the first full bloom of womanhood. They had lost two, a boy and a girl, and after talking to Twokerry, Jim Gary came to the conclusion that he wanted them back not because he loved them, but because they were his and they had been taken from him; Twokerry was a man who disliked to have things taken, whether it be a pocket knife or a child.

Burchauer was from Illinois; he spoke broken English and his wife spoke none at all. They had three children, nearly grown, but they spoke only of the one who was gone, ignoring the three they still had. Next to them, the McCandless family erected a crude shelter, and of all the people there at the creek, Jim Gary felt most sorry for Mrs. McCandless. The tragedy years before had robbed her of reason and she would sit in the sun for hours and sing to herself and her children would have to feed her and take care of her every need.

McCabe failed to return on the tenth day, and Jim Gary began to worry, not about McCabe, but about the people in the camp. They were an impatient, restless lot, always asking him where McCabe was, as though he had a crystal ball and could look into it for answers. Gary tried to reason with them, to explain that this would take time, but they did not believe him for it was something they did not want to hear. Several offered ultimatums: if McCabe did not return in five more days, they would go into the Comanche country themselves.

He had to take a stand, and he did not want to for this gave them something solid to buck, something to vent their disappointments and anxieties against. The Twokerry boy, Ralph, was the one Jim Gary watched, for Twokerry was the pusher and Ralph had just enough of the old man's antagonism in him to be the first to try to override authority.

McCabe still did not return, and time was running thin for Jim Gary; he knew this when Ralph Twokerry selected the best of the horses from their small stock, packed his bedroll, and prepared to leave camp. Everyone else seemed content to stand by and see how this would go, and Gary dared not fail, for if Twokerry got out of camp, they would all go, trampling him in the process.

Twokerry turned this into a game, bringing his horse to the edge of the camp and picketing him there; he intended to wait for the hour, the exact moment of his father's deadline, then leave, whether Gary liked it or not. And Gary studied Ralph Twokerry, trying to decide how best to handle him. Twokerry was young, in his early twenties, and the bigness of the land seemed to open the tap to his native wildness. He wore a pistol in a holster that had been pared of excess leather, and Jim Gary speculated on how good he might be. Certainly the will to use the pistol was there; the only thing that troubled Gary was the man's possible skill. If it was poor, he might succeed in disarming him, knocking him down with his fists; that would end this germ of rebellion.

But if Ralph Twokerry could shoot, and chose to shoot, Gary was not at all certain of what he would do.

Five o'clock—that was about the time. He left his own camp and walked over to where Twokerry stood by his horse. People began to gather, standing silently to watch.

Twenty yards separated the men when Jim Gary spoke. "Take your horse back, Twokerry. You're not leaving."

"Yes I am." He reached down and yanked the picket pin. "All you army men know is hurry up and wait."

Gary said flatly, "Twokerry, if I let you go, how could I hold the rest?"

Twokerry shrugged and put his hand on his pistol butt. "Kind of looks like that's your worry, soldier-boy." He grinned. "A lot depends on how far you're prepared to go to stop me."

"I thought I'd wait to see how hard you wanted to leave."

"Pa said to go," Twokerry said. "And I'm going." He drew his revolver and cocked it. "Now, you stand aside, soldier-boy."

This was, Gary decided, no different from the time that drunken corporal had thrown down on him at Fort Laramie;

35

he flipped to one side and hit rolling. Twokerry's bullet nipped dirt inches from his face, then Gary had the flap of his holster unbuttoned and was jerking his own gun free.

He shot to wing Twokerry, but the man crouched down and fired again, and Gary's bullet took him flush in the breastbone, knocking him flat. Twokerry lay there, kicking, gagging, staring with his eyes all white as though they were inverted in the sockets. With a cry, his father rushed toward him and flung himself down and lifted his son. Then suddenly he dropped the boy and snatched up the .44; he aimed it at Jim Gary and fired, but Gary rolled twice, came up with his elbows braced, both hands steadying the gun, and broke Clyde Twokerry's shoulder with one shot.

The echo of the shots dwindled to a flat, breathless silence; Gary was surrounded by a sea of shocked faces; they had not believed this could happen, could not believe it still; this was a hard, uncompromising discipline, the army kind, unapproachable, beyond argument.

Slowly Gary got to his feet and reholstered his pistol. He stood up and faced them. "Go back to your wagons. Germaine, you give Twokerry a hand. Get that bullet out of him, if you can." He singled out two more men. "Put him in a blanket. We'll bury him after supper."

The man gave him a hard-eyed stare. "I expect you'll read over him; you killed him."

"I will," Gary said. "Now you listen, you people. McCabe said to stay at the creek until he came back. So you'll stay. The army is doing all it can to see that your kin are recovered. And as a representative of the army, I'll go by army orders."

"You didn't need to kill him," one woman said. "Ain't there been enough death and heartache among us?"

Gary said, "I was the one he shot at."

He turned then, to leave them, to be alone with the sickness he felt rising, but this was not to be; his path was blocked by Jane Donovan, her brother and her father. There was censure in Sean Donovan's eyes, but he could not read any in Jane's, which gave him some small comfort.

"A bitter thing," Sean Donovan said, "that a man should have to die because he was a little foolish."

Gary pushed past him and walked on, then he realized that Jane was trotting to keep up. When they were out of earshot, she said, "I'm sorry for you, Jim. Sorry you didn't handle it differently."

He stopped and faced her. "How would you have done it?"

"I don't know, but there must have been another way. I'm

36

sure you know that and are wondering why you didn't try it." She took off her bonnet and shook out her hair; it fell over her shoulders in waves that caught the light. "Do you mind if I talk, Jim?" He shook his head. "I don't think Two-kerry or his boy ever dreamed that there'd be shooting over this. Back home, where all of us come from, we're not really punished for our mistakes, and I don't think we develop a proper respect for the severity of consequences. The first time, when we came through this country, we made mistakes, and we lost something, a life here and there, and to the ones who turned back, it broke us. Broke us inside. I know it did me, and pa. We could never accept it as a consequence of something we had done, or failed to do. So we've spent years asking ourselves how it could possibly have happened to us, or what we had done to deserve it. Poor Twokerry. The tragedy of it all was that he never knew what he was doing when he told Ralph to go. Couldn't you have told him, Jim? Told him of the consequences?" Then she shook her head. "No, of course you couldn't. I don't suppose anyone could have made him believe what he never wanted to believe. Jim, what's going to happen to us? How many of us are going to die out here?"

"I don't know, Jane. Some. Some always do." He found a cigar and lit it with hands that trembled slightly. He took a long pull on his cigar. "I'd like to be like Guthrie McCabe —hard, not caring about anything. He's the last man in the world you'd expect anything from, yet he's done more good for Texas than any man I know."

"Don't be like McCabe," she said. "Don't be hurt and lonely and afraid. Be warm, Jim. Warm enough to care and cry a little, and to keep on trying."

"Thanks," he said. "I guess I can't do anything else, can I?"

She drew his attention onto the flats by pointing. "Who's that out there? No, a little south and east. There! Is that McCabe?"

"I wish I had my binoculars," he said. They stood there in silence for ten minutes, then Gary said, "It is McCabe. Come on, we'll go and meet him."

They walked for nearly a mile, then stopped and let Guthrie McCabe come the rest of the way. He was a man bearing the mark of many miles traveled; his beard was heavy and dust lay in the creases of his clothes. Dismounting, he stamped his feet to restore the circulation.

Then he said, "Did you kill that fellow, Jim?" He laughed when Gary's mouth dropped open. "Oh, I saw it all through my field glasses. Came as a surprise, because I didn't think

37

you had the sand to stand up to a gun. I'd have let him go."

"And let the Comanches get him?"

McCabe shrugged. "It's what he wanted, wasn't it? Then there was the off chance that he'd have smarted up a little and learned how to live cold, to do his traveling at night, and not leave a trace of where he'd been." He shook his head sadly, like a father trying to push the lessons of life through his offspring's thick skull. "Jim, when you ever going to learn to let a man do what he wants to do? That fellow would have run up against his stone wall. Every man does."

"You ever hit yours?" Jane asked.

He looked at her, then smiled. "Girl, you've got your heart set on picking on me, haven't you? Do I fascinate you or something that you've got to keep prying and poking?"

"You took your own damned time out there," Gary said. "The army paying you by the hour or something?"

"A lot of country to cover," McCabe said. "And then, Sutro's horses have been swapped, strayed, and stolen three or four times." He arched his back to remove a kink; several small bones popped. "Iron Hand and I had a long talk. He's going to try to get the horses back and I'm going to take in a load of trinkets. I gave him my word that this was as far as the movers would come, and he seemed satisfied."

"The devil with Sutro's horses," Gary snapped. "Did you see anyone in the camps that was white?"

"Oh, a few. Maybe four." He scratched his whiskers. "There was a boy in Lame Bear's camp. Somewhere near fourteen, I'd judge, but it's hard to tell. Then east of there, a day's ride, I saw this girl, eleven or twelve. Pretty yellow hair and gray eyes, and wild as a deer. Be hell to bring her back."

"We'll start back in the morning," Jim Gary said.

"Whoa now! I'll go, but you stay here."

"We both go," Gary said flatly. "McCabe, I won't argue about it. I can leave Sean Donovan in charge here, or Wringle. But this is a two man job and you know it."

"All right," McCabe said. "But get it straight, Jim. If you get into a tight one, don't expect me to hang back and pull you out."

"Don't waste your worry. I know where we stand. And so do you."

McCabe pursed his lips. "Then be ready to leave before dawn." He started to step into the saddle, then paused. "Let me have the list of missing kin you've got."

"It's in my dispatch case. What do you want it for?"

"Why, I've got some matching up, don't I? And when I do, then it'll be time to talk about money."

"Just what do you mean?" Jane asked.

"Mean? What do you think I mean? How much money has your old man got with him?"

"About nine hundred dollars," she said. "If it's any of your business."

"Well, if I find a young man that fits your brother's description you're going to find out that nine hundred is my fee for bringing him out alive and unharmed." He eased into the saddle and rode on toward the camp, and Jane Donovan turned to follow him with her eyes.

Without taking her attention off Guthrie McCabe, she said, "Jim, you made a mistake today. You shot the wrong man."

7

Jim Gary was not present when Guthrie McCabe held council; he knew that he could not stand idle while McCabe stated his price, yet by staying away he endorsed the man's methods, which was worse. In his own way, Jim Gary was ducking responsibility by thinking that what he didn't see and hear didn't concern him, yet he understood that he would have to stop McCabe, and the longer he waited, the more difficult it would be.

Jane Donovan attended the meeting, or a part of it, then she came over to Jim Gary's fire and sat down. She thumped the coffeepot to see how much was in it, then helped herself.

Gary asked, "The meeting isn't over yet, is it?"

She shook her head. "I couldn't stand to look at Mrs. McCandless when he told about the girl he found. They had to carry her back to their wagon."

"You're going to see a lot of that. High hopes, then dropped and broken." He looked at her. "What was McCabe's price for bringing her back?"

Jane Donovan frowned. "The McCandless family are poor, Jim. They don't have a hundred dollars among them." She set the coffee cup aside. "Jim, you're a good man. Can't you help?"

"How?"

"You're going with McCabe. You bring her back." She reached out and took his wrist. "Jim, do you want her to live out the rest of her life with vacant eyes and a mind that understands nothing? If she could see the girl just once, maybe it would help her. Isn't it worth a try?"

"Yes," Gary said. "But as I recall, the McCandless girl had brown hair and this girl is blonde and——"

"Jim, does it really matter?"

He frowned deeply. "Jane, it's my job, the army's job, to see that all captives are returned to their rightful kin. Suppose I went along with this. Just what have I accomplished? It's like digging a hole to get the dirt to fill another hole." He raised both hands and rubbed his face. "This will never end well, Jane, I wish it would, but it won't. What could McCandless say to me? What could he say that I don't already know?"

"You could listen and find out." She got up and stood there, looking down at him, and when he could stand it no longer, he sighed and got up also.

"I'm a fool," he said and circled the camp with her to where Jake McCandless had his wagon parked. He had three walls and part of a fireplace constructed, but he seemed uninterested in building; his manner was almost listless.

He was sitting on the dropped wagon tongue and they approached his fire and stopped before he looked up, and then he moved his head slowly as though he really didn't care whether he looked or not.

"I'd offer you something," McCandless said, "but we've got nothing." He was a small man, thin in the shoulders and chest, and his skin was as coarse as cardboard.

"This is Lieutenant Gary," Jane said.

"Know him by sight," McCandless said. Then, in half apology, he added, "Got little more than a howdy for anybody these days. I've run out of talk. Run out of everything, I guess. Feel like sittin' and not gettin' up. What's the use?"

"How's Mrs. McCandless?" Jane asked.

"Same's always. She don't change much; she's either starin' or yellin'. Faints when she gets excited." He shook his head. "I'm used to it. Had ten years of it. Every time she sees a girl about Esther's age, she starts bawlin' and kickin' up a fuss. Three years ago she jumped out of a moving wagon and broke a leg." He patted his shirt pockets. "You got any tobacco, Lieutenant?"

"A cigar." He handed it to Mr. McCandless, who bit off an inch of it and chewed it. "Mr. McCandless, wouldn't it have been better if you'd stayed home? I mean, your wife can't stand much shock."

"Oh, she's tough enough, I guess. But I saw no harm in comin' back. What could I lose, with her light in the head as it is? I guess she ain't ever goin' to get better. Be a blessin' if she died. Somehow though I kept thinkin' that maybe there'd be one left over, a little girl, I mean. Not one that really belonged to anyone, but one that was left over, one no one else wanted. Lieutenant, when you live with a person for ten years, and they ain't right in the head, you understand a lot you never knew before. She ain't ever goin' to know what's real and what ain't, and if I can give her comfort in a lie, then I guess God won't kick me out of heaven for it."

"Did you talk to McCabe?"

"No use," McCandless said. "That boy he saw could be Wringle's young one. I guess Wringle will come first. Most of the others too, but it don't matter. I've spent my life waitin' on another man's pleasure. And time don't mean anythin' to my woman, Lieutenant. However, it'd please me if I could

41

get her to look at me and know me just once before she died."

"I'll talk to McCabe," Gary said. "That's all I can promise."

"Promise?" McCandless seemed puzzled. "Son, I don't ask a man to promise anything. And talkin' to McCabe won't do any good. The McCabes in this world don't listen to men like me because I've got nothing to say worth listenin' to." He shook his head and spit tobacco juice. "I got to wait and if some sunshine comes my way, then I'll stand in it until a McCabe pushes me out. Fightin' don't do any good. Resentin' it don't help either." He shook his finger at Gary. "Just one that someone's thrown away, that's all. Keep that in mind, and if she's half Injun, my wife'll never know the difference."

"Let's go," Gary said, and turned away from the fire.

Jane Donovan said nothing for a time; she walked with her arm in his. "There's nothing left in him, Jim. It kind of twists you inside when you see it, doesn't it? I mean, he'll be happy with the slops and swill of life. The part that gets you is when he thanks you for that."

"Jane, shut up." He said it kindly and simply so that she would know he was not angry with her. He stopped and put a match to a stub of a cigar; in the light his face was harshly lined, the brows pulled into a frown. "Jane, what am I supposed to do? I'm in the army. I've got to go by the book. There's no room for me to interpret the rules."

"But you will talk to McCabe, won't you?"

"Yes. I'll beg him if I have to." He laughed without humor. "That'll amuse McCabe. He likes to rub a man's nose in his weaknesses, but right now that doesn't seem important." He drew deeply on his cigar. "The trouble is, I'm afraid of McCabe, in a way. I guess all men are afraid of each other."

Someone ran past them, stopped and came back. "Lieutenant? I've been looking for you. Mr. McCabe is saddling his horse. I think he's going to leave the camp, sir."

"Thanks," Gary said. He touched Jane Donovan on the arm. "Go back to your fire. I'll see you later." He turned then and cut across the camp, casting quick glances at every fire, searching for Guthrie McCabe. He found him on the picket line, selecting a fresh horse.

Gary stopped. "Where do you think you're going?"

"Back to Tascosa." McCabe did not bother to look around when he spoke. He pulled the cinch tight and dropped the stirrup. Then he turned to Gary. "Don't get humped-backed with me, Jim. I'll be back in a week or ten days." He waved

42

his hand toward the grove. "You think that's going to mean much to them? Now step aside so I can mount."

Jim Gary did not move. "This business here is more important than any you could have."

"What the hell do you know about my business?" He laughed. "I made a date with a lady and I just about have time enough to get back and keep it."

"Anson Miles's wife?"

Guthrie McCabe stared for a moment, then shrugged. "I guess you see more than I gave you credit for. But fortunately, Anson is not so bright." He put a foot in the stirrup and reached for the saddle horn. "Ten days, Jim. You can wait that long."

Because he was confident, McCabe made a mistake; he ignored Jim Gary, who unflapped his holster, whipped out his long-barreled pistol and whacked McCabe over the head with it. The big man sagged to the ground and the horse shied, stepping away from him.

"Reese! Cassidy!"

The two men appeared on the heels of Gary's shout; they saw McCabe and stared at him.

"Get him across that horse and tie him there. Reese, have my horse saddled and a pack horse loaded with trade goods. McCabe and I are leaving right away."

Gary ran to his own fire and from his bedroll he took a pair of elkhide shot gun breeches, an extra blanket, and his rifle. Jane Donovan saw him and came over.

"Where are you going? Did McCabe leave?"

"We're both leaving. I hit him on the head. When he wakes up, we'll be miles from here."

She was more worried than displeased. "Jim, was that the right thing to do?"

"How the hell do I know?" he snapped. "When I try to do right it turns out wrong. Anyway, I felt like belting him, so I did." He gathered his gear to leave, then turned to look at her. "Jane, you're a damned pretty woman and I never seem to get around to telling you that. Trouble is, I'm always in a hurry. Wish I had more time."

"Take time."

"Just so you don't forget," he said and put his hand on the back of her neck. He pulled her against him and kissed her. When he released her she stood close to him, not touching him, but very close and the clean scent of soap rose from her hair and he could almost feel her body warmth.

"I'll be back," Gary said and walked away.

Gary ran toward the picket line. Cassidy was there with

the horses; the pack horse was tied by a lead rope, as was McCabe's horse. Gary stepped into the saddle and slid the rifle into the boot.

"You're sure in a hurry," Cassidy said as Gary lashed his roll behind the saddle. "What'll I tell Wringle?"

"Tell him good-by," Gary said and left the camp, crossing the creek a hundred yards down where there was no quicksand.

An hour south the land began to change, opening up into gullies and rising into distant ridges. The brush was becoming more dense and now and then a jack rabbit startled him by dashing across his trail. A breeze pushed dead brush along, and lifted dirt into a swirl. Gary tipped his head back and studied the sky, dark, starless, a black cap for the world.

McCabe's groan stopped him, and he waited while McCabe was sick.

"Untie me," McCabe said.

"Can you behave yourself?"

"I'll beat your goddamned head off for this."

"Then you'd better stay tied." Gary nudged his horse into motion, knowing how painful this was for McCabe; a man is not designed to ride belly-down on a saddle.

A hundred yards later, McCabe said, "All right, all right! Have it your way."

Gary dismounted and untied McCabe, who would have fallen to the ground had Gary not caught him. There was a welt on the side of McCabe's head, and before he could think to do anything about it, Gary lifted the pistol off him and kited it into the brush. This enraged McCabe.

"I paid fifty dollars for that!" The burst of temper pained him and he pressed both hands to his head. "God damn you, Gary. This is something I'll square with you."

"After we get back," Gary said flatly.

McCabe suddenly became aware of his surroundings; he whipped his head in four directions, then stared at Gary. "What the hell is this anyway?"

"Army business first, Guthrie. All right, we're riding, and if I have to use the spurs, I will."

"You're not tough enough," McCabe said. He sat down, head pillowed in his hands. "God, my head's full of hammers." He sat that way for a moment, then looked up at Gary, who was a vague blackness surrounded by the inky night. "All right, you want to go into Comanche country, then we'll go. But I won't guarantee you'll get back."

"I didn't ask for any."

McCabe grunted, then pulled himself erect, using the stirrup for support. "Jim, it's a big country where a man can cash in almost anyplace. Don't expect anything from me—a favor, help, or advice." He grinned. "Why should I sweat to give you some lumps? I'll let you make your own mistakes. What about my gun?"

"What about it?"

"Be hell to find it in the dark, that's what about it."

"You just lost your gun," Gary said and mounted. He sat there, waiting for McCabe to pull himself into the saddle. Finally he said, "I don't enjoy your company. But this is something I've got to do, Guthrie. I've got to be a sucker; I can't help myself."

He turned then and rode on, staying now to the higher ground, following the crest of one ridge to the next. There was no talk between them, no trust, no friendliness, and this filled Gary with misgiving. They camped in a pocket, picketing the horses in some nearby brush, but Gary couldn't sleep; he lay in his blankets, shivering in the dawn chill, watching Guthrie McCabe, listening to him snore. He was afraid, and that was bad enough, but McCabe made it worse just by knowing he was afraid. Knowing it and enjoying it like a spectator enjoys a fight with one certain outcome.

8

Through the next day's travel, Guthrie McCabe did not speak once to Jim Gary, but every time Gary turned his head and looked at McCabe, the Texan smiled faintly, as though he enjoyed a private joke. For his evening camp, Jim Gary chose Chino Creek, and without consulting McCabe, he built a small fire and put on the skillet to heat. This brought McCabe out of his silence. "You want to call Comanches? It'd be easier to holler."

"I'm not trying to hide," Gary said. He mixed some flour and water, added a little starter, then cooked the wheat cakes. Pushing some sowbelly toward McCabe, he said, "You can slice that."

"No knife."

Gary gave him his. When the hotcakes were done, they folded them around the strips of sowbelly, and ate while the coffee boiled in the frying pan. Finally Gary said, "Just when I think I'm beginning to understand you, you do something stupid, like wanting to ride back to Miles's place. Has she got her hook into you that bad, Guthrie?"

"Her?" He laughed. "Don't be a fool."

Gary shook his head. "McCabe, you've lost your mind." He held the cup between his palms and leaned forward. "You know what I think? I think you're the loneliest man in Texas. Your favorite song is that you never do anyone a favor, but I think that's a damned lie. You're always doing something for someone, but you're covering it up with a lot of selfish talk, like you were ashamed to be human. You know something, Guthrie? You like to have people owe you. It makes you feel real good to have people in your debt, even when they don't want to be. I'm wise to you, so I won't ever owe you. With me, you've got to pay your way, and I don't mean to buy it either."

"Jim, you're real mixed up about me."

"No, I've got it straight. Guthrie, the thing you want is a friend who likes you because you're Guthrie McCabe, and nothing else. But you've been kicked so hard, by your pa, and by Miles, that now you think that no one would ever like you for yourself. That makes you afraid. You want to stick out your hand, but you're afraid one more man will snap at it." He got up, threw the coffee into the fire and then scraped dirt over it until it was out. "Let's ride."

McCabe stared at him. "What's the hurry?" He continued to watch Gary, then after a moment, he got up and brushed off the seat of his pants. "All right, let's go then. God damn a man who likes to be the boss all the time."

Gary laughed. "You just can't stand to be told what to do, can you, Guthrie?" He felt pleased with himself, less fearful, for with this knowledge of McCabe's character came weapons, to turn his will, to make him angry; Gary found that he had strings to pull and that McCabe would react.

"I've had enough," McCabe said and took a swing at Gary. There was only time to duck, and even this upset his balance so that he fell backward, with Guthrie McCabe launching himself to keep him from getting up. Gary was partially rolled out of the way when McCabe landed, and then Gary felt McCabe's hand fumbling at his holster, trying to unbutton the flap, to take possession of the pistol.

Gary hit him alongside the head with his elbow, then McCabe jerked away, the pistol in his hand. Quickly, Gary grabbed for the frame and cylinder, locking it tightly, which prevented McCabe from cocking the piece and firing it. They came to their knees, both struggling for the gun, both tugging, resisting, trying to wrench the other free of it.

Somehow, Gary managed to trip McCabe; when he fell, his grip on the pistol relaxed and then Gary stepped back, covering him. His breathing was ragged and he looked steadily at McCabe, who sat on the ground, braced against stiffened arms.

"You want this badly enough," Gary said, "I'll make you eat it, barrel first."

"Don't get sore," McCabe said. "A man's got a right to try."

He partially turned, then came erect with a rush, his hand stabbing for the gun as Gary pulled the trigger. To his surprise, the pistol failed to discharge, then McCabe cried out in sudden pain; he danced about, clutching his left hand, and strangely, the pistol dangled from it, flopping about as though it were invisibly fastened.

Gary grabbed him and held him, and McCabe quieted, but he was hurt.

"Get it off!"

He held up his hand and Gary saw then what had happened. By grabbing the gun, McCabe's hand had gone too far and the hammer had fallen on that web of flesh between the thumb and forefinger. The pointed firing pin had gone clear through the flesh, preventing the cartridge from being ignited. Cocking the gun again, Gary freed it from McCabe's

47

hand and let the hammer down before dropping it into his holster.

The wound bled badly and McCabe clutched his wrist, his face chalk-white. "Jesus that hurts!"

"Let me look at it."

McCabe jerked away as Gary reached for his hand. "You get the hell away from me! You've been nothing but trouble to me." He stripped off his neckerchief and bandaged the wound tightly. Pain was still biting him; it put a saw-edge in his voice, and a pinched look around his mouth. "Let's get out of here before you kill me."

He walked over to his horse and climbed into the saddle. Then he sat there, bent forward, head down, nursing his pain. Gary almost tried to help him again, then decided to let him alone; he packed his gear, tied it behind the saddle, then mounted.

"You can lead on from here," he said. "This is as far south as I've ever been. We'll try Iron Hand's village first."

McCabe nodded and led out. He kept his shoulders rounded and Gary studied him as they moved along. The wound was painful, he knew, but he could not help but wonder which pained him worse, the wound, or the knowledge that he had been bested by a lesser man. McCabe was sensitive to things like this; he believed that he walked above men, and over them when the notion suited him, and a licking from any man would be hard to take.

I was lucky, Gary told himself. But maybe the next time I won't be.

Iron Hand's camp lay a half a day beyond the dawn and they sighted it when the sun was high. They made their approach in the clear and rode through the racing children, with the dogs snapping at the horses' heels. Two hundred penny-colored faces stared at them as they moved between the stinking lodges toward the center of the village. Both men dismounted there and Gary took picket pins from his saddlebag and tethered the three horses. Guthrie McCabe stood with his left hand tucked into the front of his shirt, turning his head now and then to watch the outfringe of women and children. The bucks formed a ring around them, their expressions gravely neutral, neither savage nor friendly. War was too fresh a memory to allow them open trust of any white man, even Guthrie McCabe.

Jim Gary took off his pistol belt and hung it on the saddle-horn as a gesture of peace. Then Iron Hand came from his lodge, robed, beaded, poker-faced. One hand was hidden as he approached them, his copper face inscrutable.

Iron Hand spoke remarkably good English, then Gary recalled that he had once gone to an Indian school. "McCabe returns as he has said, but he brings a stranger here to my fire."

"He is a trader from the north," McCabe said.

Iron Hand thought about this for a moment, then he saw that Gary was unarmed, and decided it was all right. "What do McCabe and the trader seek?"

"A place by your fire," Gary said. "The hand of friendship."

"Will the trader accept my left hand of flesh, or the right which gives me my name and has no warmth?" He exposed his hand, which was a leather cuff laced high on the forearm. A bent piece of polished steel formed a hook.

"I will take the cold hand in peace," Gary said, "for it gives you the name, Iron Hand. That name is known where all men walk."

This flattery pleased the Comanche and he smiled through his eyes. "Come to my lodge," he said and turned away.

In a soft voice, McCabe said, "You can talk like a horse thief when you want to, can't you?" They followed Iron Hand, then he waved his hand and a woman rushed forward with a bowl of food. The odor suggested dog meat, and a lot of other ingredients best not thought about, but Gary ate it and nodded in appreciation, which he felt not at all.

In Indian fashion, Iron Hand let time pass, and a lot of small talk before he came to the main issue, the reason for their visit. "The winter will be severe, McCabe, and my people have not hunted well this year. The horses of Sutro have not been returned. Perhaps more gifts——"

"We'll speak of that later," Gary said. "The third horse bears gifts."

He wondered if he would be impolite if he looked around the camp, then decided not to risk it. Under the guise of looking for the horses they might be permitted to remain a few days; there would be plenty of time. Still he wondered how the subject could be switched from horse trading to slaves; perhaps McCabe had an answer; he seemed full of them.

Iron Hand was speaking. "I do not live alone on a mountain top. The horses will be returned, then we can speak of trade." He paused. "If I could see the goods, I perhaps might find the horses sooner."

"Three men may unpack the horse," Gary said.

A signal from Iron Hand sent them scrambling, fighting to be the first to unlash the pack. McCabe gave Gary a disapproving glance, but dared not say anything. Watching the In-

49

dians—he had an excuse now—Gary noticed a tall young man who kicked and bit and cursed his way through the milling group. The young man was as brown as a nut, yet his hair was light, and when he turned his head, Gary saw that his eyes were gray. He judged his age to be fourteen, although it was difficult to tell when they grew up wild. Other than the hair and eyes, the white blood had been bred out of him, leaving him pure Comanche in thought and action.

Iron Hand seemed satisfied with the quality of the goods, and the talks resumed, mostly lies told by Iron Hand in an effort to convince them how honest he was, how he lived with honor and had never stolen a thing in his life. They sat through the speech, then listened to different braves swear to the lies; Gary let this run in one ear and out the other. This took all afternoon and much of the night and Gary began to understand that nothing would be settled that night. He got his blankets off the horse and lay down by the fire.

The next day he wandered about the camp unmolested. Iron Hand had made an attempt to find the horses because the Comanche was smart enough to know that if he failed to produce them, the gifts would stop. Yet Iron Hand was an Indian, proud and vain, and he would never admit that any member of his village had taken the animals; he went through a long rigamarole to "find" the horses. Iron Hand claimed that the horses had been stolen by someone else and that members of his tribe were trading for them and that he would have to give many buffalo robes, but as a gift to the two white friends, he would hand them over. Still there was some hedge in Iron Hand's talk; he kept referring to the bad winter coming, and how valuable a horse would be, and the more he talked, the more convinced Jim Gary became that he was about to hit on something, like an easy way to switch the talk and the trading for white captives instead of Sutro's horses.

He wanted to talk this over with McCabe, but the man kept wandering off, clearly indicating his preference for being left alone. Gary walked about, looking for the white boy, and found him, with his coup stick and war-making implements; the Comanches always practiced war, even when they talked peace.

A direct query was out of the question, so Gary passed out some cigars among the women, and loosened a few tongues. He knew enough of the language to understand them. Yes, the boy was white. He had been taken quite young; the woman could not remember when exactly, but the boy was the faithful son of Lame Bear and had counted coup against the white soldiers before he was ten.

50

This was, Gary assumed, Wringle's son. Now his job was to get him out of the Comanche camp as peacefully as possible. A trade might be in order, yet Gary did not feel in the least cheered by this. He had watched the boy and now wondered if he could lead such a wild animal back to his rightful parents. Then there was the matter of keeping him, teaching him those thousand subtle things a young man had to know to be even halfway acceptable to society.

Right then, at that moment, he saw that Guthrie McCabe was right; this whole business was a mistake. It should be left alone, a thing over and done with and best forgotten.

But he knew it wouldn't be that way.

9

There was nothing in Jim Gary's nature that made waiting easy, yet it was something he had to do now, and with all the outward signs of enjoying it. He could not help but worry some about Wringle and how he was making out at the Sand Creek grove. The responsibility for the civilians' conduct and safety was Gary's, passed on to him by Colonel Frazer, who hoped to hold this balance for another few months, then get out of it completely. Now Gary had passed it on to Wringle, who really could not be held accountable at all if anything went wrong.

By dark, no one had returned to Iron Hand's camp with Sutro's horses, and during the evening meal, Gary spoke of this to McCabe.

"I'm getting tired of waiting. Let's press Iron Hand now and make the best of it."

McCabe shook his head. "Been looking around some and we'll have to play this cozy. Iron Hand will fetch the horses, when he's ready, then we can talk. He'll want to keep the horses. After he argues we'll offer an alternative. That boy could be Wringle's."

"You've been thinking the same thing I have," Gary said wryly. "I thought I was one jump ahead of you."

McCabe smiled. "That'll be the day." He motioned with his head. "Tonight, wander around and see what you can see."

"What do you think I've been doing?"

"Wake up," McCabe said. "You've seen what they want you to see. Get away from the camp. Go to the water hole, or where there's wood to be gathered. If a Comanche's got a slave he doesn't want you to see, he'll keep him in the lodge during the daytime."

"All right. Where will you be?"

"With Iron Hand, shooting the bull."

"That's a soft touch," Gary said and drank what was left of his coffee. He left McCabe with the clean-up and knew that he would resent it, but it gave Gary pleasure to sting this man. McCabe's hand was heavily bandaged, Gary noticed, and he did not use it at all. Later, Gary decided, he would make another attempt to dress it properly, if McCabe would let him. The trouble with these men who liked to do for themselves was that they usually lived in fear of appearing weak, less sufficient than they were. Gary couldn't see the disgrace in accepting help.

He had been in the Comanche camp long enough not to attract attention no matter where he went, so he eased past the last group of lodges and made his way leisurely to the creek. A fringe of cottonwood trees lined both banks, and Gary walked to the end of the trail and stopped there, a few feet from the water, his back against a tree.

His wait was long and tedious and without reward, then he gave it up and cut along the creek bank, walking nearly a mile before angling back through the trees to the camp. The night was ink and he could see nothing farther than a few feet in front of him.

He heard a twig snap ahead of him, then collided heavily with a woman; he identified her sex by her sharp gasp. She had an arm full of kindling and dropped this. Her English was precise and unmistakable. "You clumsy savage! Why don't you watch where you're going?"

"I'm dreadfully sorry," Gary said and raked a match alight, to see whom he was apologizing to. He had only a glimpse; she was strikingly attractive, large eyes, a full, curved mouth; Gary whipped out the match when it singed his fingers.

The woman stared at him, then said, "You're white!"

"I'm Lieutenant Gary. What's your name?"

"Janice Tremain." She held her hand against her side where he had bruised her. "I thought a stranger was in camp. I haven't been allowed out of the lodge in the daytime." She started to cry, then checked it quickly. "To hear someone speak something besides Comanche is more than I can——"

"How long have you been here?"

"Five years, I think. Yes, it's been five years."

"Where can we talk?"

She thought a moment. "We'll go bathing in the creek."

"What?" He was quite shocked.

"It's the custom for couples to bathe. No one will bother us. Besides, it's dark and if we go upstream a few yards——"

Gary said, "I've never done this sort of thing."

"Then we can stay here. This path is well used for wood gathering, and some squaw is bound to come along. She'll see us and tell Stone Calf. Then he'll try to kill you."

"Stone Calf?"

"My husband," she said simply.

"My God!" Gary said. He wiped a hand across his face. "I think the creek is the lesser of the evils." She pushed past him then and he followed her to the water's edge. Farther downstream, someone splashed water and giggled, then a buck slapped his chest, or something, and there was another

53

burst of delighted giggling. Janice Tremain looked at Jim Gary, then untied the drawstrings to her simple dress and shed it. His intention was to turn his head, yet he did not; he had a moment's glimpse of a firm, well rounded body, then she waded into the creek until the water reached her shoulders. He heard her laugh, then she said, "At least take off your boots, Lieutenant."

This embarrassed him, and he shed boots, shirt and trousers. Hang the underwear, he thought, and went into the water with her. Within moments, a half-dozen couples were bathing, each keeping a respectful distance from the others. Moving close to him, Janice Tremain said, "If a woman wants a lover, they bathe together. And if the angry husband bursts upon them, both can say that they were only washing. It saves his face."

"Forget the customs of aboriginal tribes," Gary said. "How the devil did you get here in the first place?"

"A stage was attacked," she said. "I was going to join my father at Fort Elliot."

"That's my post!"

"I'm an army brat. My father was Captain Tremain. Is he well?"

For a moment Gary couldn't place the man, then he remembered the talk; it had all happened before his assignment at Fort Elliot. "I don't have time to soften it," he said. "He's dead."

She did not cry or betray emotion. "I'm glad. I wouldn't want him to know me now. How did he die?"

"He took his own life."

She nodded. "I thought it was like that. He was a man of honor, and was touched deeply by many things. He withstood pain well, but he was easily broken by grief. When my mother died he——"

"Janice, do you want to get out of here?" He asked the question abruptly, almost as though he feared she might say no.

"It's all I've thought of, but I'm not sure." She shivered and crossed her arms over her breasts. "I have no children; that way I'm lucky. But they know I'm barren and Stone Calf has another wife who bears his children. So life hasn't been easy for me here. They've worked me hard."

Gary said, "You must have relatives."

"An uncle," she said. "Senator Tremain." She touched his arm. "I've been gone too long now. Stone Calf will come looking for me. I'll meet you here tomorrow night."

"I may be gone by then," he said. "Janice, let me take you back."

"Let me think about it. This is so quick, meeting you, finding hope again. Tomorrow night? Here?"

"All right," he said.

She waded ashore then and he waited until she was dressed before leaving the stream. Quickly slipping into his clothes, he meant to follow her, then let the idea go; he might invite danger by such an action. Danger to her.

He returned to the main camp and McCabe's fire. The Texan was rolled in his blankets, but he turned around as Gary sat down.

"I met a white woman. Been here five years. Guthrie, I'm going to get her away from here."

"Wait a minute," McCabe said. He looked around to see if anyone was within earshot. "This wouldn't be Stone Calf's wife, would it?"

"She's Janice Tremain," Gary said. "A white woman."

"Yeah, yeah, and Stone Calf is Iron Hand's brother too." He settled back and pulled the blanket around him. "You leave her alone, Jim. I don't want the Comanche nation down on my neck."

"You knew she was here?" He was incredulous.

"Sure. Don't look so damned shocked. Stone Calf took her when he raided the stage. There's a hands-off sign on her. Make sure you read it right."

There was a lot he wanted to say, even an anger to express, an anger at the sudden knowledge that politics invaded so basic an act as freeing a white woman prisoner. An army brat at that. Gary felt almost honor bound to rescue her.

McCabe, he knew, regarded him as a wide-eyed innocent that no amount of experience would temper, and Gary supposed the Texan was right in his judgment. Yet he felt no shame because he was this way; he did not consider it a character flaw.

During the past few days, he had been impatient to leave. Now he wanted to stay a day and a night longer, just so he could meet Janice Tremain again, to help him decide which way he should go—his own, or Guthrie McCabe's. If he went McCabe's way, Gary supposed that he would never be able to forget her, and his desertion. Yet he would live with it, if he had to. Most men had such things to live with.

The horses were produced the next evening, along with Iron Hand's long-winded account of how they were borrowed by mistake, and how much he had to give to get them back. Both McCabe and Jim Gary listened to this; it was all part of the game a man played when he dealt with Indians.

Talk of trade began, and Iron Hand set his price high,

55

often reminding both McCabe and Gary that horses were most valuable with a cruel winter coming on. McCabe played his game shrewdly, trying to lower Iron Hand's price while the Indian held it as high as he could.

Gary wondered how long this would go on; already they had talked for two hours. Then McCabe pulled the switch, suddenly, without warning: he offered to trade all the goods Iron Hand had asked for the horses for the yellow-haired boy.

McCabe could be persuasive, Gary discovered. His argument was strong: a man could hunt buffalo with a horse, but a boy made poor riding when it came to hunting.

This called for a conference; the Indians drew to one side, and McCabe put a match to his cigar.

"We'll get the boy," he said softly.

"You sure?"

"Yes. Iron Hand will kick up a fuss, but he'll see it our way." McCabe rubbed his jaw. "Now to figure out how to get him back. These are the only folks he remembers. Probably have to tie him to the pack horse."

"I'll put our gear together," Gary said and left the fire. He rolled their blankets and stacked them near the fire, then went to the picket line on the pretense of looking at the horses. After wandering about for a moment, enough so the guard no longer paid any attention to him, Gary ducked away and ran for the grove of trees near the creek.

He stood around for a few minutes, listened to several couples already in the water, then slowly walked up stream to the spot where he had met Janice Tremain the night before. She was not in sight and Gary began to fret; he had no time to waste.

Then he heard someone splash in the creek, and took a chance. Undressing quickly, he went into the water and found her at midstream.

"Running Wolf brought the horses back," she said. "When will you leave?"

"Very soon. Will you come?"

"I'm afraid now. But not for myself."

"You must come, Janice. I'll see that we cross the creek farther up. Be waiting." He took her arm and shook her. "Janice, it's now or never. There is no other way out."

"All right." He started to leave; time was pressing him like a hand at his back. She touched him and he turned back to her. "What will I do? It's been five years."

"Let me take care of it," he said. He knew what she meant, how she could explain five years and yet remain socially ac-

56

ceptable. Rashly he said, "Janice, let me take care of everything. Do you understand? Everything."

He left her then, dressed and returned to McCabe's fire; the Texan was ready to leave. The boy was mounted and bound, firmly tied to the horse, and somewhere in the camp a woman wailed and threw ashes on herself for she had lost a son. McCabe saw the dampness of Gary's clothes and only frowned.

"Let's go," he said, stepping into the saddle. He was a bit awkward with the reins, being able to use only one hand, and Gary knew that it pained him badly, for mounting had jarred it and McCabe's expression was strained.

"I'll lead," Gary said, tying the lead rope to his own saddle-horn so that the boy rode between himself and McCabe. Iron Hand raised his hand in a token of peace, all the while congratulating himself on the slick horse deal he had made.

Gary made certain their exit was casual, but he glanced back often to observe the boy, who sat stone-faced, only his eyes alight with hatred. In his mind, Gary speculated on whether or not there would be an attempt to rescue the boy, then he decided there would not be. Iron Hand was too dependent now on the white man's favor; the next step would be to herd them to a reservation. So Iron Hand would restrain the boy's foster father. His thief's instincts would be held back, this time.

McCabe said nothing until Gary turned and started to cut across the creek close to the cottonwoods.

"Hey, that's the wrong way!"

"Shut up," Gary said.

He edged his horse closer, then Janice Tremain ran from the woods and came up to him; he took her hand and she put her foot in the stirrup, mounting behind him.

McCabe swore softly, then said, "You did it now, you damned do-gooder! We'll be dead by sunrise."

Once away from the camp, Jim Gary increased his pace in order to put as much distance between himself and Stone Calf as he could; he knew that an hour might be all he could gain; he dared not hope for more. He rode double and was slowed by the boy who already fought his bonds, and McCabe was riding humped in the saddle, his hand giving him trouble; Stone Calf would have very little difficulty making up that hour.

They had to stop, or kill the horses, and Jim Gary hated the thought of either. He dismounted and helped Janice Tremain down. A glance at the sky assured him that dawn was yet some time away. Then he looked at McCabe and found him standing near the boy, who remained tied to the horse.

"I'll watch him," McCabe said softly. He spoke to the boy in Comanche and the boy spit at him, earning for his effort a slap in the face.

"Cut that out!" Gary said. He started toward McCabe, then let it go and sat down beside Janice Tremain. "How much time have we got? The truth now."

"Before Stone Calf misses me?" She shrugged. "I would say that he's left the village." She folded her hands together. "Actually, I think he will be glad to get rid of me, but pride will make him follow."

"Will pride make him come alone?"

Janice frowned. "He might. But he has three young sons. They might come with him in the name of family honor."

"We'll have to figure it that way then." He got up to get his canteen and offered it to her first. "You're not sorry?"

"No. Just frightened." She looked at Guthrie McCabe. "Who is he?"

"McCabe. Haven't you seen him before?"

She shook her head and he opened his mouth to tell her about the man, then decided to let her judge for herself. Besides, this was neither the time nor place for judgment.

He walked over to McCabe. "Stone Calf is probably behind us. Got any ideas?"

"Leave her here," McCabe said. He fumbled in his pocket for a cigar, found one, then put a match to it. "She's got no business with us, Jim. When you going to stop doing favors for people?"

"She's white. And she's army."

"That may be enough for you, but not me." He shifted his injured hand, trying to find a more comfortable way to carry it.

"That beginning to bother you?"

"I can live with it." He looked at the boy, who sat silently, his attention seemingly somewhere else. "I think he understands what we're saying."

"So?"

"So that makes him doubly dangerous." He rolled the cigar to one corner of his mouth. "Jim, when we started, I told you I wouldn't stick around and pull you out of any holes you got into. You going to give the woman up?"

"No," Gary said.

"Damn, but you're stubborn." He shrugged. "All right. I'll say good-by now, and likely I won't see you back in camp."

"Are you running out on me?"

"Depends on the point of view. Like the little kid holding the cat's tail; the cat does all the pulling. Me, I'm leaving because it's a good way to stay alive. Still I wouldn't set you up for Stone Calf. You take my horse. I'll go on, riding double with the boy." He reached out and tapped Jim Gary on the chest. "Look, this will be better for you. And don't get the idea you can stop me. Stone Calf will have his sons with him, so hitting me on the head would only increase your troubles, not solve them."

"Thanks for nothing, you bastard," Jim Gary said.

McCabe was amused. "I am, ain't I?" He clamped his cigar firmly between his teeth and swung up behind the boy, reaching around him for the reins. "I'll travel fast and straight, Jim. You'd better take the roundabout way. There's some badlands about twenty miles from here. Good for holing up during the daytime."

In spite of himself, Gary said, "I'll give you my rifle. You'll need a gun."

McCabe shook his head. "Stone Calf will be after you, not me." He started to lift the reins, then thought of something else. "You're mad at me, Jim, and I guess you think you have a right to be, but I told you some time ago how it would be. It occurs to me that I could get shot in the back as I leave, but then I guess you're too much of a gentleman to do a low thing like that."

He drove his spurs into the horse's flanks and rode out, the hoofs clattering as he drove down the draw. Then the sounds faded until Jim Gary could hear nothing and he was filled with an immense sense of loneliness.

Janice Tremain came over. "Where is he going?"

"His own way. McCabe always goes his own way."

"He's leaving us?"

"Yes," Gary said.

He took her arm and led her to McCabe's horse, boosting her into the saddle. "We've stayed here too long. McCabe was right about that."

He led the way and she followed him closely, but they did not speak; he was inclined to silence and she was observant enough to see that, and respect it. Perhaps she was also observant enough to sense his misgivings; his decision to rescue her had been spontaneous, hasty, and possibly regrettable. Yet he was also the kind who finished what was started; he seemed terribly determined not to make any mistakes.

There was in Jim Gary's mind the sure knowledge that he was only an adequate man who continually overreached his native ability; he was not brilliant or brave or even outstandingly resourceful; his record at the Academy and his service sheets proved that. Given a job, he would do it, but he could never rise to greatness because greatness was not in him. He was sorry now that he had taken Janice Tremain from the village; the coward in him caused this regret, for her presence placed him in personal jeopardy. Yet his instincts, his training, forbade leaving her—his conscience and sense of duty grappled for the upper hand.

He could even envy McCabe for his lack of conscience, the selfishness that permitted him to do what was best for himself and never think of others.

From behind him, Janice Tremain said, "It's not too late for me to turn back." She said this because she felt she owed him this much, but the thought of turning back pained her, forced her to add, "The worst that can happen to me is a beating."

"Be daylight in five hours," he said. "We'll be in the bad-lands by then."

Somewhere off on his left flank, McCabe would be pushing through the night with the boy; Gary wondered how much Wringle had promised to pay McCabe for the safe delivery. Enough anyway to make McCabe strike out on his own rather than stay and risk losing the boy. This was something else that troubled Gary, his failure to prevent McCabe from fleecing the civilians. Colonel Frazer liked to have his orders obeyed, and Gary would have to report complete failure. Wringle might be willing to pay, as would some of the others, but there were some in the grove who knew the world owed them a handout, and they would file a complaint against the army, which Frazer did not want at any price. He wouldn't get his brigadier retirement and Gary wouldn't get his

60

captain's "railroad tracks." And the civilians wouldn't get what they wanted either. Just McCabe, who was tough enough, and smart enough, would get it all.

The first rinse of dawn found them in a barren waste of jumbled rock and gorges. This was a breathless, lifeless, forgotten land, and somewhere in the back of Gary's mind he remembered hearing that the Indians had deep superstitions about the place; they avoided it unless desperately pressed by their enemies.

They hid the horses and stretched out to rest, but there was no lasting shade. As the sun climbed, the cool shadows disappeared and a molten heat lay trapped, making breathing a chore. Gary tried to sleep; he was bone-weary and his eyes burned and the unshaved stubble on his face itched, but he could not rest.

Finally he sat up and tipped his hat low over his face. Janice Tremain tried to use the horses for shade, but they kept moving about, so she gave this up.

She unlaced the front of her dress to the waist and let it hang loosely, trying to keep reasonably cool. Gary glanced at her once, then studiously avoided looking at her again. He did not want to think of her as immodest; he supposed five years as the common wife of a Comanche had caused her to forget for a moment that she was a proper lady, an officer's daughter.

"Who commands Fort Elliot?" she asked.

"Colonel Frazer. He's up for retirement soon."

"I don't know him. What will I say when I go back?"

"Tell them you're glad to be back and let it go at that," Gary said.

"Yes, a man could say that, but not a woman." She tried to do something with her hair, to brush it with her fingers, but it was long and ungroomed and unmanageable. Her complexion was dark from exposure to the sun, and her fingernails were broken and split from difficult work. Her dress was thin buckskin, all she had to her name; she lifted the hem of it, looked at it with disdain, then let it drop as though she did not want to think about it any longer. "I was engaged," she said softly. "He was a junior officer at Fort Elliot. Lieutenant Culver. Perhaps you know him."

"Hardy Culver? He was transferred to Fort Yuma three years ago." He turned his head and looked at her. "His wife went with him. She was going to have a baby."

His desire was only to tell her the truth so that she would not show disappointment before anyone, yet his words hurt her deeply; he observed the tightness of her cheeks, the sudden, drawn thinness of her lips.

"If you're going to say you're sorry, then don't," she said. "What did I expect anyway?"

"A world that hasn't fallen apart," he said.

She turned her head slowly and he saw tears in her eyes. "Yes, that's exactly what I expected. And why isn't it that way?" Her voice rose in volume, in anger. "Why is it that it's all happened to me while everyone else goes off scot free? Am I being punished for something I don't know I've done?"

Along the pathway of Jim Gary's life there were strings of hurt birds, homeless, small animals, all lovingly nursed, and it was natural for him to put his arms around her and hold her against him while she wept over the unspeakable injustices of living. He understood her fears for they were real. Somehow the world was always too busy to offer sympathy; she would find very little of it at Fort Elliot. Sure, they would have a dinner in her honor, and everyone would be polite to her, but that would wear off and they would soon be wondering how many lodges she had shared and in time the commanding officer would politely question her presence on the post; after all, she had no direct connection with the army; they could not keep her because of a dead father and a fiance who had quit grieving and married another.

"Strange, but I thought there were no more tears." She did not look directly at him when she spoke. "Sooner or later I'll have to stand by myself, so we'll make it sooner." Perspiration ran down her cheeks and stood out in small globules on her upper lip. "I think that's what frightens me most, the fear that I won't be able to stand by myself and look anyone in the eye who asks me what it was like to be a female prisoner. Jim, if I falter just once, I'm through. Do you understand what I mean?"

"Yes," he said. "I know exactly. We're alike in that respect, Janice. Destroy our equilibrium even in the slightest, and we're totally lost. I guess that's why I'll be army and nothing else; I feel secure in the protocol of the service." He smiled then.

She said. "If—if you could be by me, Jim, just at first, I know I'd be all right." This was only a hope on her part, a hope she knew was faint, for he had his duty and that came first. "I'm sorry. I've asked too much of you already."

"We'll work it out," he said and got up, climbing high in the rocks to view the back trail. The sun smashed down, raising rippled heat. He turned his head and spoke to her. "McCabe has a pair of field glasses in his saddlebag. Would you bring them up here?"

She found them and climbed to where he lay, stretching out on her stomach beside him. He took the glasses, adjusted them, and spent many minutes carefully scanning the distant flats.

"Nothing," he said, genuinely puzzled. "I don't see anyone." He raised the glasses for a more thorough look, then put them aside and shook his head. "I don't understand this. From here I can see ten or twelve miles. Stone Calf ought to be out there somewhere."

"Could it be that he didn't leave camp?"

"No, no," Gary said. "We've got to figure the worst and prepare for it. And I keep thinking of McCabe, who knows Comanches damned well and he was worried about Stone Calf. No, he's out there all right, and I'd give six months pay to know just where."

11

By mid-afternoon the heat in the rocky pocket became so oppressive that Gary put aside his caution and decided to leave, hoping that sunset would catch them on the edge of the flats. Frequent search with the field glasses netted him nothing; he saw no sign of Stone Calf or his sons. Still, Gary could not believe that the Comanche had given up, or that he had not bothered to pursue them.

They walked down to the lower levels, leading the horses, and Janice Tremain did not speak; Gary was not sure whether it was the heat and weariness that made her withdraw or her thoughts of going back to civilization. The first night they had met, he had promised to help her and it was a promise hastily given, a promise he might not be able to keep. Another failure. Only this bothered him more than the others; like most men who lived on the edge of failure, he was very sensitive to it.

Gary was careful working his way down to the flats, and he took his time, trying to think ahead in the event he was walking into an ambush. Having left the highest ground, he had no vantage point from which to survey the terrain and spot his enemy; he could only blunder on now, pitting his intelligence against the practiced hunt-craft of the Comanches.

By his judgment he had another hour among the rocks, another hour of soft footing along with the nettle sting of fear-sweat on his face. He could not make up his mind where safety lay, in a quick dash across the flats, or waiting for darkness, then taking a roundabout route. Either way he would leave signs that Stone Calf could follow. Either way, the Indian stood a good chance of catching him, and killing him.

At the last fringe of rocks, Jim Gary hunkered down and took out his field glasses, carefully searching the flats before him. He saw nothing and put the glasses away.

"We'll go straight north," Gary said, his decision made. "By my reckoning, the Fort Elliot patrol will be out there somewhere. I'd rather look forward to them for help than the civilians in the Sand Creek camp." He uncorked the canteen and offered it to Janice first, pulling it away when she tried to drink too much. "That water has to last another fifty miles. A swig three times a day, that's all we can afford."

"He didn't come for me," she said softly. "I don't know whether I'm happy or insulted." She wiped her hand across her face, leaving dirt streaks. "Don't look at me like that, Jim. I've shared his blanket for five years. Do you want me to feel nothing?"

"I don't know what I want," he said. "We'd better go."

When he stepped near her, she took his arm, turning him to face her. "Let's be honest, Jim. The thought of me with an Indian fills you with fury, doesn't it?"

"Yes," he said. "God, Janice, you were born for a white man!" He realized how stupid that sounded, yet he had spoken his true feelings, revealed to himself another facet of his personality that he had only suspected before. He stood there, shaking his head back and forth. "I guess it all boils down to the fact that I'm white and I'm better."

"Are you, Jim?" She asked the question because she wanted him to find the answer for himself, not give it to her.

"I want to do the right thing," he said.

She smiled at him, then said, "Jim, don't we all?"

He put her on the horse, then turned to his own as a rock skip-clattered down the side of a nearby rise. Gary whipped his head around and caught a glimpse of doom; Stone Calf had his rifle leveled and Gary reacted, flinging himself down, letting the bullet smash into the neck of his horse. The animal screamed and went down, then Stone Calf discarded his single-shot rifle and bounded off the ledge, knife flashing, his throat filled with war-cry.

Gary had enough time to regain his feet and meet him, hand grabbing for the wrist, fending off the knife. Even then it bit slightly into the flesh of his shoulder, driving him to renewed strength.

The two men stamped about, boots drumming the dust, trying to lock legs, trip each other. They fought breast to breast, cheek to jowl, sweat and spit and hate blending, then one fell and they rolled, arms and legs beating the barren ground, grunting at each other as though this were an animal language that both understood.

Gary did not know when he turned the knife, or how he did it; he only felt it bite deep, then he threw his weight on the bent wrist and drove it deeper. Stone Calf cried out, then fell back and Gary got unsteadily to his feet and stood there looking down as though he had just killed something horribly untouchable.

Janice Tremain cried out and vaulted off the horse; she rushed to Stone Calf and lifted his head. He was dying and the knowledge was in his eyes and his last strength was spent when he lifted his hand and brushed her cheek.

65

"Stone Calf—comes alone," he said. Then his head rolled and his eyes assumed a vacancy and she slowly let him down until his hair mingled with the dust.

"He kept me alive because he favored me," Janice said softly. "What can I do for him now?"

"Forget him," Gary said. "The past is truly dead now."

"Yes," Janice said.

Then she knelt by his head and began to chant, the Comanche death song, and she rocked back and forth and threw dust in her hair while Jim Gary watched with mounting horror.

"Stop that!" he shouted.

If she heard him she gave no sign and he moved toward her.

"In the name of God, I tell you to stop!" He pushed her, then struck her heavily in the face with the back of his hand. She fell and looked at him and he saw that she was crying and this enraged him completely, possessed him, insulted him; he was immeasurably offended because she felt emotion toward an Indian. "I wish to God I'd never brought you away if you loved him so much!" He whirled away and mounted his horse. His instinct was to leave her there, but he cooled his anger, forced himself to speak civilly. "Get mounted, Janice."

"Why?" she said, rising. "Why should you take me back, feeling as you do? Because I'm white and you think each kind should be with his own?"

"Something like that," Gary said. "I don't think trying to explain it will help anything. Not now."

"No. We'll never understand each other."

She pulled herself into the saddle behind him, never once looking back at Stone Calf as they rode into the growing darkness.

Three hours after Guthrie McCabe parted company with Jim Gary and Janice Tremain, he stopped and told the boy to dismount. Leaving him tied hand and foot, McCabe built a very small fire and cooked a meal. The firelight flickered in the boy's eyes, and he watched McCabe carefully, noticing the injured hand, measuring the Texan as though figuring out the odds of escape.

McCabe was aware of this scrutiny, and spoke in Comanche. "You might as well forget it. I'm two jumps ahead of you."

"You are without weapons," the boy said. "And your hand is in pain."

"A kid like you I can handle with one hand," McCabe

66

said. He picked up a stick of wood. "Try anything and I'll break this over your head."

"Your heart can be cold. But it can be warm, and that is weak." He smiled. "You were kind to the other white man, but it will do no good. Stone Calf will follow the horse carrying double for but a short way, then know that you have tricked him. He will know that I would not be taken into the badlands."

McCabe's manner was one of respect. "Smart kid, you are. All right, but I bought Gary and the woman some time. It was the best I could do."

He offered the boy something to eat, feeding him with his fingers rather than untie him. McCabe's injured hand was nearly useless and the slightest movement caused him intense pain. He had not looked at it for a day, but it was badly swollen and it ached continually so that he found sleep difficult. The boy was a man by Comanche reckoning, and because of this, McCabe respected the danger he represented. And the boy saw more than he let on too.

McCabe got up. "Get on the horse. We're getting out of here."

"And let Stone Calf see the fire?"

"Something like that."

The boy laughed. "Stone Calf is a man of many summers, very wise. He will find the woman and take her from the white man and leave his bones to bleach in the sun."

"That could be," McCabe said. "We'll see."

He tied the boy to the horse, making hard work of it with one hand, and then the boy flipped out his knee and bumped McCabe's bad hand. A sunburst bloomed in McCabe's skull and he fell to the ground, crying out, writhing, and the boy dashed off, wheeling around, guiding the horse with his knees.

Before McCabe could gather himself and mount, the boy had a hundred yard start in the wrong direction, but he began pursuit while a hammer tormented his skull and his hand flamed.

The boy made a game of it, yapping like a noisy dog leading another in play; he raced around McCabe, who was afoot and helpless.

McCabe yelled; "Does the Comanche teach their young to run like a woman or to count coup?"

This was a desperate chance, and the boy took the bait, wheeling the horse to ride McCabe down, to touch him before riding back to his village to boast of the deed. At the last possible moment, McCabe whipped aside and flung out his arm, catching the boy in the stomach. He knocked him back, spooked the horse and set him to bucking, thrashing the boy around like a stick on the end of a string. McCabe lunged again for the bridle, caught a trailing rein, then had the horse and prisoner again under tow.

He wanted to rest a moment, to nurse the pain in his hand, but he dared not show further weakness to the boy; he was as wild as any animal and infinitely more dangerous. Mounting behind him, McCabe said, "You have your fun?"

"Dancing Bear is too old for games. I will kill you."

"Sure you will," McCabe said. "Or maybe get yourself killed." He gigged the horse into motion and tried to ease his hand so that it pained him less.

The way he figured it, the hurt hand was just something that had to be; he took his chance on getting shot, so he couldn't really complain about the hand. In life, a man had a lot of kicks hurled at him and he ducked as many as he could and did not cry about the ones that connected.

He decided that when he got back to the movers' camp on Sand Creek he'd bathe the hand in hot water and take out the soreness. But after he'd delivered the boy and collected from Wringle.

McCabe wore out the night traveling, and when dawn came, the boy spoke. "Stone Calf has killed the white man by now. He will take the woman back to his lodge and beat her properly."

"You know something? You're not worth all the bother I'm taking with you." The boy turned and looked at him, his pride injured. Indian fashion, he wanted torture, brutal treatment; it was a value of his worth as a man; only women and children were killed quickly or disregarded.

"Yes, sir," McCabe said. "You're just a snot-nosed kid who ought to have his ass paddled. Now when you get among your own people, you act right, you hear?"

"I am a Comanche!"

"You'll never be Indian," McCabe said. "No more than Stone Calf's wife is Indian." He sighed. "Damn it, boy, what am I going to do with you anyway? Don't you remember anything about your real folks?"

"I am a Comanche," the boy said.

"All right, all right," McCabe said in English. "Jesus, why can't people leave a thing alone anyway? Poke around, stir it up, shake it, cry about it; they'd be better off if I turned you loose. But I can't even do that, boy. Too late for that."

68

12

Guthrie McCabe remained near the Wringle wagon, not because he wished to be sociable, but because he smelled trouble, and wanted to avoid it if he could. It seemed that everyone in the Sand Creek camp was congregated around Wringle's wagon, and they stared at the boy and pestered him with talk he did not understand.

He was frightened and trying not to show it; he believed that he had been brought here to be tortured, then killed; this was what he would have done had one of them fallen into his hands. Wringle and his wife were pathetic; she cooked a meal for the boy, a homecoming meal that had been long planned and was the best she had, and he picked up the laden tin plate and threw it in her face. Wringle did not know whether to hit the boy or forgive him; he touched him and the boy seized his arm and bit it deeply; Wringle retreated, blood dripping from his fingers.

From McCabe's elbow, Jane Donovan spoke; he had not heard her approach; he was not sure how long she had been standing there. It was easy to come and go in this crowd. "Can't you do something?"

"What can I do?" He looked at her. "Wringle's got to handle this his own way."

"Speak Indian to the boy. Make him understand."

"He understands," McCabe said. "I talked to him on the way in." He hunched his shoulder, trying to position his hand more comfortably. "Wringle's got to understand that he's made a mistake, having the boy returned. He'll never tame him."

"How much did he pay you?"

"Enough," McCabe said. "You want the exact amount?"

"No. I know what heartbreak costs." She paused. "Where's Jim Gary?"

"With a woman he found." McCabe waved his hand. "Out there some place, trying to stay alive."

Wringle was talking to the movers, asking them to leave because they made the boy nervous. He might as well have spoken to the night, for they remained around his fire, their eyes curious, each wondering if this would be happening to them. Even Mrs. McCandless was there with her vacant, wandering eyes; she studied the boy and when he saw her, his attention remained on her like a magnet.

"Someone ought to get her out of there," McCabe said. "The boy has been raised by Indians and they don't like anyone who's sick in the head."

"What happened to your hand?" Jane asked curiously.

"Hurt it."

Wringle's wife was moving slowly toward the boy, speaking softly, smiling, trying to touch his heart with words. He waited until she was within reach then pounded on her, bore her to the ground, his hands locked in her hair, trying to drub her head against the earth. Wringle and two men pulled him free, then Wringle picked up a strap, raised it, and finally dropped it and stood there with tears running down his cheeks.

"I've seen enough of this," McCabe said, turning away.

Jane moved with him. "Come to the wagon. I want to look at that hand."

At her fire she heated a kettle of water and McCabe removed the bandage from his hand. He had to jerk the last bit, ripping off a scab; puss drained from it and his face was chalky from the pain.

Jane lighted a lantern so she could see better; her expression tightened when she saw the wound so badly festered. She used a salt and boric acid solution in the water and when she pushed McCabe's hand into the pan, he gasped, then clenched his teeth.

"What will Wringle do with the boy, McCabe?"

He looked at her for a moment. "You change the subject mighty fast when you get the notion." Then he shrugged. "Let him go. He can't keep him. The boy was taken too young. Maybe they'll learn from this. I hope so."

"Is that why you brought the boy back, so this would happen? So they'd all see and give it up?"

"It was in my mind," he said. "But you always hope that this one will be different. It never is. How long do I have to soak this?"

"Until I say it's enough. The hand is infected. You want to lose it?" She made him rest the hand on a towel while she reheated the water.

"Are you sure this is Wringle's boy?" She studied him when she said it. "You're not really sure, are you, McCabe? Here, put your hand back in the water."

He ground his teeth together for a moment, then said, "There's a good chance the boy is Wringle's, but who can be sure? What difference does it make anyway? None to Wringle. If I'd brought in a monkey with the hair shaved off, it would have been the same. A long time ago he made up his mind that he'd do anything, take anything, just to get his boy back. That became an excuse, a password with Wringle. God knows how many failures it's covered."

"You don't feel pity for him," she said. "Just disgust." She dried his hand, then took out a sharp knife and heated the blade.

"What are you going to do with that?"

"I'm going to cut that open so it'll heal."

"Oh, no! They way you feel you'd push that extra deep."

"What would it matter? I couldn't touch your heart." She leaned forward and looked steadily at him, her eyes large and bright in the firelight. "Do you want to lose the hand? You know I'm not lying to you, don't you? Let that hand go and you'll lose it, maybe the arm. And Guthrie McCabe couldn't live with one arm; he'd be half a man."

"You're as hard as a man. As hard as I've ever seen." He took a cigar butt from his pocket and lit it. "Go ahead and cut. But don't expect me to yell."

"Naturally," she said and made the incision quickly, deeply.

McCabe's eyes were like white eggs and the cigar dropped from his mouth, then he fell over, the cigar burning a hole in his vest until she flicked it away. Her father came up as she was putting a bandage on McCabe's hand. He looked down at the Texan and asked, "He sleeping?"

"He fainted."

"The hell you say."

Donovan filled a cup with coffee then squatted until she finished. She made a sling for the hand, then said, "Help him over to the wagon. Liam can get his bedroll."

By cutting north and keeping up a steady march, Jim Gary hoped to intercept the Fort Elliot patrol, and his luck ran well for he sighted it late in the afternoon of the third day, a thin column reaching across the flats, a dark line moving sluggishly with only the guidon to mark the head of it.

Gary emptied his pistol into the air and listened to the report soak into the immense miles, then he saw the column increase its pace and change direction slightly, bearing down on him.

Captain Winslow Scott was commanding, a razor-jawed man in his middle forties. He dismounted, leaving the detail in the charge of the sergeant, then took off his hat and bowed when he saw Janice Tremain.

"In heaven's name, Gary, where did you find her?"

"Iron Hand's village. Janice, may I introduce Captain Scott? Janice Tremain, Captain."

A look of awe and wonderment came into Scott's gaunt face. "Not old Pistol Britches' daughter? Sergeant, on the

71

double here." He put his arm around Janice's shoulder, a completely unnecessary gesture for she could have out-marched him any day of the week. Yet she permitted him this; it was a gallant part men like to play and she did not wish to deprive him of it. "Sergeant, have the detail dismount and light squad fires."

"Here, sir?"

"Damn it, you heard the order. Take Miss Tremain with you and see that a shelter is erected to protect her from the sun."

"Really," Janice said, but Gary's touch closed it off.

"You're back in the army now," Gary said. "Go with the sergeant. Everything will be all right."

"Of course it will," Scott said. "Get on with it, Sergeant." He then took Gary's arm and led him a dozen yards away so their talk would not be overheard. "The old man is on needles and pins; he hasn't received a report from you."

"I've been busy."

Scott smiled. "Indeed you have. She's a looker, isn't she, in spite of the Comanches." Then his gaiety faded. "Has McCabe made any progress?"

"One boy was recovered."

"Just one?" Scott frowned. Like most men in command, he wanted everything done yesterday. "I'll have to include that in my report, Gary, and I don't think the colonel will take it well."

"Hang the colonel!"

"Here, here. The heat's getting you, Gary. Damn it, we all have our job to do. If it wasn't you doing it, it would be someone else." He offered Gary a cigar, and a match. "Tell McCabe to work a little faster. These civilians are an impatient lot. We don't want them complaining of army in-efficiency to their congressmen. A thing like that could go down the line and land on some first lieutenant's neck."

He turned his head and looked at Janice Tremain, who was sitting beneath the newly-erected shelter, a canvas stretched on four poles, the back side of it staked to the ground to block out the smashing sunlight. "She may save your bacon, Gary. Her father was well known in the army. Does she have any relatives?"

"Some politician."

"Ah, yes, I recall now. I'll dispatch a man to go on ahead and send a wire. Naturally I'll mention your name."

There were no good-bys in Gary to say, but to avoid un-pleasantness, he walked over to the shelter. "You're in good hands now, Janice. Good-by."

72

She stood up and he noticed absently that she was nearly as tall as he was.

"I'd embarrass you if I kissed you, wouldn't I?"

"Yes."

"I won't then." She offered him her hand. "You've been most gallant, Jim, and I'm sure you've done the right thing, as far as the army is concerned."

"What does that mean?"

"Anything you want it to," she said. "Will I see you again?"

"Perhaps, if you remain at Fort Elliot."

"You know I can't do that." She let her shoulders rise and fall. "You'll have to forgive me for not thanking you for bringing me from something to nothing. With Stone Calf, I had a halfway home, but all that's gone now so I can go back to no home at all. My father, my fiance, even Stone Calf are gone. So I can't really thank you, can I?"

"No," he said.

"All those years I dreamed of getting away, but now I no longer want it. Good-by, Jim." She turned away from him with the abruptness of a closed door; he stood rooted for a moment, then stomped angrily to his horse.

In passing, Scott said, "All the details are not clear in my mind, Gary."

"What details, sir?" Gary stopped.

"You know what I mean. The circumstances under which you found her ought to be included in the report."

"She was gathering firewood. I asked her if she wanted to go back and she said yes."

"Is that all?"

"Yes, sir," Gary said. He mounted and turned out, moving in a southerly direction. Behind him, Scott yelled something but Gary ignored it completely and kicked the horse into a run. He did not pause for nearly a mile, then when he stopped and looked back Scott had the detail mounted and moving toward Fort Elliot.

The sight saddened him, not because he was alone on this immensity, but because he had done what was right and had it come out wrong. Wrong for Janice Tremain. Had he left her with Stone Calf, he supposed she would have always thought of going back, just as the civilians at Sand Creek wanted something they didn't have. But time would have softened this for her, made her content with her lot. That was, Gary decided, the key to being happy, to be satisfied with what you had and to keep the wishing just what it was, wishing.

13

The last thing Jim Gary thought he would see on the prairie was three wagons moving north; he spotted them at dawn and rode toward them, unable to understand why they were there.

Silas Barnstalk had the lead wagon; he drew up as Gary wheeled his horse around. Barnstalk's wife, riding inside the wagon, looked out, saw who it was, then pulled her head in, no longer interested.

"What's the matter?" Gary asked.

"We've had enough," Barnstalk said. "That's what's the matter." Two men dismounted from the other wagons and came forward on foot. They looked at Gary but said nothing, just stood there with their hands tucked into the bibs of their overalls.

"Did McCabe get back with the boy?"

"Boy?" Barnstalk laughed without humor. "By God, a mountain cat would be more like it. Wringle's having one hell of a time. His woman's thrown up her hands and won't go near the kid. No, we seen that and that's enough. My Jess was three when we lost him. Be seventeen now. If that's what he's like, the Comanches are welcome to him." He motioned to the other men. "Lige and Sam feel the same way."

Sam Ludlow said, "Wringle's wishin' now that the boy was back with his people."

"All he'd have to do is turn him loose," Gary said. "The boy'd skip out during the night."

"Funny you'd say that," Barnstalk said. "Wringle's turned the boy loose, but he hangs around. Seems like he's watchin' something, waitin' for something." He took out some cut plug and worried off a chew.

"When you get to Fort Elliot, try to tell this to the new folks living by the creek."

"Another batch, eh?" Barnstalk laughed. "Well, I won't be going to Elliot, Lieutenant."

"Well, good luck to you anyway."

"Same to you," Barnstalk said.

Gary mounted and waited while the wagons filed past him, then rode on toward Sand Creek. He wondered how many of the others would be following Barnstalk. A good many, he hoped. The more that gave up, the better it would be.

Besides, they'd all given up before, and that sort of got to be a habit with some men, getting easier each time.

But I don't want it to happen to me, Gary thought.

Another night on the prairie, then he saw the grove before noon, and entered the Sand Creek camp while the sun was high. He thought the place oddly silent; people stood around in clannish groups, not working much, and talking less. He saw the boy near Wringle's wagon, sitting in the shade, staring at a spot of ground between his outstretched legs.

Gary went on to the Donovan camp and found Jane there. She was washing the midday pots and dropped them with a clatter when she saw him. Gary put his arm around her and walked with her to the fire.

'Haven't had a decent cup of coffee since I left," he said. "Where's McCabe?" His voice assumed a flatness when he said the man's name and Jane's eyes took on a questioning expression.

"In our wagon." Gary forgot about the coffee and unflapped his pistol holster; Jane put out her arm and stopped him. "McCabe's flat on his back, Jim. His hand became infected." She took his arm. "Come on, sit down. You look like you rode to hell, measured it, then rode back." Her hands pushed at him, then handed him the coffee cup. "Let's talk, Jim. Then you can do what you think you have to do."

He tried the coffee, then smiled. "Man, that's good. Real good."

"McCabe said you had a woman."

"I took her north and met the Fort Elliot patrol. She's army."

"Oh. It's good to be somebody, isn't it?" She squatted down across from him and watched him. "You look good to me, even with the whiskers." She lifted the pot. "Better have a refill on that coffee before pa and Liam get back."

"The camp seems unusually quiet."

"It's Wringle's boy," Jane said. "Nothing has been right since McCabe brought him back."

"I met Barnstalk on the way in. Lige and Sam were with him."

"There'll be others going. It doesn't take much to discourage them, Jim."

"And you?"

"I wouldn't want to go back."

"Winter's five months away," Gary said. "What about your brother?"

She shrugged. "I hope he's dead. I hope McCabe or you never go back and bring another into this camp. I've seen

75

enough, Jim. I think all of us have, but some don't want to admit it."

He got up and walked over to the back of the wagon and looked in. Guthrie McCabe was stretched out on a pallet of folded blankets, his hand a pillow of bandages.

"Heard you talking," McCabe said. "You caught me when I'm down, Jim."

"What I've got is good enough to keep until you can stand."

"Now you're sore. I see you made it. The woman in camp?"

"The army's taking care of her."

"I'll bet she likes that," McCabe said. "Do me a favor and roll up the sides of the canvas top. It's like an oven in here."

"Kind of gives you a taste of what hell is like," Gary said, but he rolled the sides.

Jane was cooking some backfat and beans for him; he again settled by the fire. "He's been a better patient that I thought he'd be," she said.

"Why not? He can't help himself. Yet." He looked around the camp. "Wish a fight would start. The quiet gets you, doesn't it?"

"Jim, why doesn't the boy run away?"

"I don't know." He took the plate from her and began to eat, but he had hardly cleaned up half of it when someone yelled in a long, drawn out wail, then a sudden and mixed shouting came from the other end of the camp.

Gary dumped his plate and started to run even as a crowd gathered around the McCandless wagon. He used his elbows and fists and battered his way through, then stopped quickly, having come to the inside of the perimeter.

The boy was there, glaring at them, an animal ready to pounce at the first sign of antagonism. Mrs. McCandless was there too, on the ground, her normally vacant eyes now made permanently so by death. Gary saw the stout stake, carefully sharpened, the butt protruding from her chest, and he knew that the boy had killed her, although it seemed completely senseless at the time.

Around him was utter silence, shocked silence. McCandless was there, looking at his wife, then at the boy. This seemed to be a signal, for the crowd suddenly vaulted into action, roaring, yelling, driving forward, grabbing the boy, beating on him with their fists as though he were a demon representing all the accumulated hurt they had known in their lives.

Gary tried to stop them but they mowed him down like a new reaper in a field of wheat; he rolled and thrashed to keep from being trampled beneath their feet. Suddenly they were free of him, moving away, the boy suspended above

76

their heads, gripped by a dozen angry hands. They were a roaring, savage animal mob and the boy's screams rose above the sounds they made.

Gaining his feet, Gary staggered after them, drawing his pistol, then remembering that he had not reloaded it after firing the signal shots at the Fort Elliot patrol. He tried to use it as a club, to knock men asprawl, but a few turned on him and took it away from him; he was completely helpless against them.

Someone produced a rope and they threw it over the limb of a tree while others fastened the loop around the boy's neck. Eager hands hoisted him aloft and he jumped like a toy on a string, his eyes popping, tongue bitten through. His hands clawed at the rope around his neck and the man on the other end began to jerk on it, making him jump and swing while they yelled their hatred and let spit run from the corners of their mouths.

Gary could only stand there and watch and listen until the sawing parted the strands of the rope and the boy fell like a shot bird. Instantly the yelling ceased; it was like water pouring from a ruptured dam, at last finding a sane level, leaving only a trickle now in place of a torrent.

The boy was dead and they lost interest in him, turning away, going back to their wagons without a word. Only one man remained, Wringle, who looked at the boy and silently wept, then in time he too turned away, to get a shovel to dig the grave.

Wringle saw Gary standing there, and said, "I wanted my boy back. That's all I wanted. A man must have a curse on him to have all this happen to him."

"I'll get some help for you."

"No. He's mine. I'll bury him. Let each bury his own."

Gary went back to Jane Donovan, sick, sorry, ready to give the order to pull out; couldn't they see by now how it was? He was surprised to find McCabe leaning against the wagon; he was very weak and Jane was trying to help him back inside, but he stubbornly resisted her.

"They killed him?" McCabe asked.

Gary nodded. "Not the easy way either. Like animals."

McCabe became angry then. "God, if I'd suspected, don't you think I'd have warned McCandless?" He wiped a hand across his sweating face. "Indians fear anyone who's not right in the head. Evil spirits live there. Usually they kill off their own when they're that way. The boy did what he thought he had to do." He let Jane help him sit down. "When I heard the first yell, I had that feeling. Then I remembered how the boy looked at Mrs. McCandless the night I brought him into

77

camp. But it was too late then." He saw Gary's torn clothes, the blood on his face from the cuts he had received during the struggle. "I can see you tried to stop them. You could have got yourself killed."

"But at least I tried."

McCabe accepted the coffee Jane handed him, then sat with the cup in his hand. "Jim, be smart and call it off. Pack 'em up, kit and caboodle and take them back to the fort."

"You know I can't do that."

"What's to be gained by staying? Didn't Stone Calf chase you and the woman?"

"Yes."

McCabe frowned. "I'm afraid to ask the next question."

"Then I'll save you the trouble; he's dead."

McCabe groaned, but not from pain. "Jesus, that's Iron Hand's brother." He drank his coffee and handed the cup to Jane. "Help me in the wagon. I want to lie down; I feel sick all over again." He leaned on Jane's arm, then crawled over the tailgate. She came back to the fire and stood there for a moment.

She shuddered. "How could anyone ever live in such a country?"

He raised his head and looked at her. "You just live and forget about the rest."

She waved her hand in the direction of McCandless' wagon. "How can you ever forget that? I think it ought to stay with you as long as you live."

"Did you think for a minute that it wouldn't?" Gary asked. He left her then, went to his horse and took off the saddle-bags. At the creek he bathed, soaked to soften his whiskers, then lathered his face and shaved; he seemed to find comfort in this simple, familiar task.

McCabe was probably right; the best move would be to get out of the country before Iron Hand let his medicine man work him into the mood for war. Sooner or later someone would trail Stone Calf, his sons probably, and when they found what the buzzards had left, they'd be mixing paint and loading cartridges.

By going back to the fort, Gary supposed that he could gain a temporary reprieve from Comanche wrath, but if he hadn't bobbled in the first place there wouldn't be any reason to go back. And what would going back really solve? The civilians would still be howling to the politicians for their loved ones and the army would have the job of recovering them.

He'd have to come back anyway, do the damned job all over again, so he decided to stay and figure a way out of this. If he failed it wouldn't matter because the army would have a hell of a time court-martialing a dead man; if he won there wouldn't be a need for it.

There were no certain odds on a thing like this, Gary decided, but he guessed that he ought to go to Iron Hand and have a talk. The possibility occurred to him that if he said the wrong thing he might end up head down over a slow fire, but he surprised himself by not being frightened by this prospect.

"You made your bed," he said to the creek. "So now you sleep in it."

14

Jim Gary read the brief funeral service over Mrs. McCandless, and everyone in the grove was there except Wringle, who had reading of his own to do. After the headboard had been set in place, McCandless shook Gary's hand and thanked him.

"She's at rest now. Poor woman, she's had a heavy load to carry these years." He looked past Gary, past the last fringe of wagons to the lone man and his own mound of earth. McCandless' eyes pulled into fleshy slits, and his expression grew thoughtful. "Don't seem right that a man should have to stand alone over his only son; there's something indecent about it." He stepped around Gary and walked slowly toward Wringle.

McCabe, who stood by Jane Donovan, said, "Help me over there."

She looked at him oddly, almost joyously, then gave her arm for support. He was not a well man, not strong, but he was determined, and closed the distance without faltering.

Jim Gary looked at the others. "Anyone else? Or aren't you big enough?"

They knew what he meant, but not one budged, although the desire to do so was evident in their eyes. Gary understood how it was; one man stepping out would have broken the invisible hold on them, but there was no man willing to take that first step. Finally he turned and walked over to Wringle and the mound of earth.

McCandless was looking at the crudely carved headboard. Then he said, "In a way, neither knew what they was doin', Wringle."

The other man nodded. He kept his head tipped forward as though studying the brass eyelets in his shoes. "Everything was against him from the very start, wasn't it?" He took out a handkerchief and blew his nose. "When I was a kid I used to spend time cryin' when the cat would have a litter. Out of five or six only one would live. The others would get stepped on by a horse, or run over by the reaper, or killed by dogs. I guess the Lord figures we're animals too, 'cause there's so many of us who got to get killed off and there don't seem to be much we can do about it."

"I'm sorry," McCandless said. "Sorry for my woman and your boy, and plumb sorry I went crazy like I did." He put his hand briefly on Wringle's shoulder and walked back to his own wagon.

"I suppose you'll go back now, Mr. Wringle," Gary said.

After a moment, Wringle said, "I guess not. I'm going to build, right here. Right here on Sand Creek." This was, Gary guessed, more than an idle boast or a spur-of-the-moment statement; Wringle meant it. He put the shovel on his shoulder and went back to his camp.

Gary and McCabe stopped by McCandless' wagon. McCandless said, "Nothing for me here now, but if Wringle can stay, so can I."

"Go back to where you came from," McCabe said flatly. "For once in your life, be smart."

"Who wants to be?" McCandless asked.

At evening time, several more families broke camp, made up their wagons, and announced their intention of leaving this forsaken country. Jim Gary did nothing to stop them. They left early in the morning; just before sun up, a quiet departure with no good-bys; they just pulled into a string and started north across the prairie. In an hour they were only vague dots against the heat shimmer, and soon after that they vanished.

Gary likened this land to the sea, with its changing moods and unforgiving character; a man could easily vanish on its face and leave not a trace.

He wanted to talk to McCabe about Iron Hand and the advisability of remaining at Sand Creek, so he went to Jane Donovan's wagon and found her alone. McCabe, she told him, was at the creek, bathing. He walked downstream to a thicket of rushes, guided the last twenty-five yards by splashing and off-key singing. McCabe jumped when Gary parted the rushes and sat down on the bank, then he relaxed and went on with his bath.

Gary said, "You feeling better?"

He canted his head and looked at Gary. "Still carrying a grudge?"

"It can wait. Right now I need some advice. What's Iron Hand going to do?"

"Froth at the mouth. Dance and sing songs and tell everyone how the white man lied and double-crossed him." McCabe got out of the water and dried himself on an old blanket. "And you did, Gary. I told you to leave the woman alone."

"This is all my fault?"

"You took the woman and killed Stone Calf." He slipped

81

into his underwear and pants. "Of course he'll blame me because I brought you into the camp as a friend. McCabe's name is mud now."

"The honor is richly deserved," Gary said.

McCabe laughed. "What's going on in your do-gooder mind now?"

"I've decided to go back to Iron Hand. I don't know how, but I've got to make him listen, to understand that I was forced to do what I did."

"He'll take the hide off you a layer and an inch at a time. Then, in a week or so, if you're still alive, he'll cook your brains out over a slow fire." He slipped into his shirt and buttoned it with one hand. Putting on his cartridge belt was more of a chore, but he managed it, even to tying down the bottom of his holster. "Jim, what makes you so stupid?"

"I work hard at it," Gary said, determined not to rise to McCabe's bait.

"You're stubborn as well as stupid," McCabe said and stepped past him. His right side was hidden from Gary and McCabe sneaked the draw on him, cracking the young man heavily on the head with the barrel of the gun. Gary wilted instantly and blood oozed from the long split in his scalp.

McCabe wiped the barrel on his pant leg, then reholstered the pistol. He looked down at Gary and shook his head. "God damn it, you're the hardest man to do anything for. You go into Iron Hand's village and you're dead, and you're too damned pure to die. There aren't enough like you as it is."

He left him lying in the rushes and walked back to the grove, thinking that it would be better if he just saddled up and rode out without saying anything to anyone. Still, he couldn't do that; he'd have to speak to Jane Donovan; he felt compelled to say something, give her some reason.

She was washing clothes, boiling shirts in a kettle when he came up to the fire. "Too hot to do that," he said.

"Hot or not, they get dirty. Where's Jim?"

"At the creek," McCabe said. "I came to say good-by."

She frowned and deserted the washing. "Why?"

He let his shoulders rise and fall. "Because I've had enough too. I'm getting out."

"No, that isn't what I meant. Why say good-by to me?"

"Because you're the first woman I haven't—well, worked for something. Or maybe because you hated me, yet treated me like you'd treat Jim Gary."

"I could have changed my mind about you, Guthrie."

"No reason to," he said. "Given a chance, I'd still lift the pennies off a dead man's eyes." He looked at her and found her regarding him carefully; he pulled his glance away.

"Don't be afraid of people anymore. They won't hurt you." Jane held out her hand.

"Yes they will. But it's worth it." He dropped her hand— quickly. "Look, when you see Jim again, tell him good-by. Tell him that I like him in spite of things I've done and said to him."

He turned away from her, then stopped and looked back. "Jane, why don't you marry Jim Gary? I mean, he's your kind of man, Jane. When you're both old you can look back at the mistakes he's made, but you won't feel a damned bit ashamed at any of them."

She opened her mouth to speak, but he wheeled and went to the picket line, there saddling his horse.

There wasn't much of a plan in McCabe's mind, except that he couldn't let Gary go to Iron Hand's village; they'd kill him before he could state his case. Still, McCabe knew that he himself would hardly be welcome; Indians did not single out men to blame for their troubles; they blamed them all; took out their hate on those handiest, usually some inno- cent traveler who died wondering what the hell it was all about.

"I'm a no-good bastard," McCabe said to the horse. "And now I want to do one thing that will make people remember me without getting mad."

Still he was a man who calculated his chances carefully; he fully believed that he could get away with this, and return to Sand Creek alive, with his ears still fastened onto his head. The chances were there against it, but he never backed away from a risk or two. The thought occurred to him that this might look better than it really was, and there was enough recalcitrant rogue in him, enough schemer, to make him thor- oughly enjoy this—a moment of genuine heroism.

He spent the night on the prairie, huddled in a split in the earth, sleeping with one ear cocked, his horse saddled and picketed close by. He was a lone man in a lonely land and his mind kept going back through the years to other times when he had felt like this. Like when he lived under Anson Miles's thumb in the mansion, jumping when Miles told him to jump, and hating every minute of it.

He was riding hours before the sun came up. In the after- noon he came on Iron Hand's camp and rode boldly into it, through a quickly gathered avenue of hostility, then he stopped before Iron Hand's lodge.

The Comanche came out, looked long at Guthrie McCabe,

then raised his hand but a brief inch. Instantly the braves howled and converged on him, sweeping McCabe clean off the horse.

They hoisted him aloft and carried him into Iron Hand's lodge.

15

Bertha Stokes, who was nine and unable to stay out of the creek, found Jim Gary moaning in the rushes; this frightened her so she ran and brought her father, along with four other men in the camp. They carried Gary back to the camp; he was too sick to help himself.

The cut was bathed and bandaged, and he slept through the night while Jane sat outside, quickly coming awake every time he stirred. By morning he was left with only a throbbing headache and a renewed anger at Guthrie McCabe. He left the wagon and had breakfast with the Donovans.

"He's gone," Jane said. She spoke quietly and this drew Gary's attention.

"All right, tell me where."

"I'd have to guess," she said. "But I think he went to see Iron Hand." She looked at her father and brother; they said nothing, just scooped food off their tin plates.

Gary looked at each of them, a frown building on his forehead. "No, he wouldn't do that. That would be a dumb thing to do, and McCabe does only the smart things, the things that are best for McCabe."

"I saw the direction he took," Liam Donovan said. "This time he wasn't heading toward Fort Elliot."

Gary's interest in breakfast vanished and he got up, walking back and forth, his lip caught between his teeth. "I was going to go. We talked about it before he slugged me with his gun."

"He didn't want you to die," Jane said. "Can't you see that?"

"I can see what it looks like, but it's not McCabe. He doesn't do things that way."

From the other side of the camp, someone yelled, "Ri— durs! Riders coming!"

Gary walked across the grounds and stood on the north side where a group gathered. His field glasses were with his blankets, but by shielding his eyes with his hand he could make out a four man detail, unmistakably army.

"Stay here," he said and walked out to meet them; this would be army business and he didn't want everyone listening to it.

Sergeant Goldman was in charge, a whiskered man with a large cud of tobacco in his cheek. He saluted before dismounting and handed the reins to the man on his right.

"Dispatch for you, sir," Goldman said, producing it. "I met Captain Scott five hours out of Elliot. He told me where to find you. Hurt your head, sir?"

"No," Gary said. "This keeps the sun off." He ripped open the envelope and read the message, then swore. "What the hell does this mean? Report back to Fort Elliot immediately! By heaven, I've got enough trouble here without——" He cut the rest off and blew out his breath.

"I wouldn't know that, sir. I talked with Scott and he'd sent a rider on ahead to telegraph that Tremain woman's uncle. You know how those politicans are, sir. Likely he sent a wire to Colonel Frazer, and now you get your orders."

"But I'm needed here!"

Sergeant Goldman shrugged. "I guess a politician is more important."

"Sergeant, I just can't go!"

"Lieutenant, you'll get court-martialed if you don't." He wagged his head. "In twenty-four years I haven't yet figured out the way the army runs, but I just do as I'm told and let the fellow higher up worry about it." He turned to the detail. "Dismount. We'll start back in a half-hour, if that suits you, Lieutenant."

"Yes. Hell, yes. Let's go if we have to." He turned and walked back to the creek where the civilians waited, the question on their faces. He suddenly saw that they did not trust the army. They depended on it because they had to, but they did not trust military policy. And he hardly blamed them.

"Find Wringle and send him to the Donovan wagon," Gary said and passed on through.

He hurried back to the Donovan camp; they stood there. "Liam, would you roll my gear and saddle a horse for me?"

"Sure," he said and left the fire.

"What did the army want?" Sean Donovan asked. "Some change in plans? We ain't been ordered out?"

"No, but I've been ordered back to Elliot," Gary said. "Not for long though. I ought to be back in ten days." He was not sure of this, but it sounded good, made them feel better. Wringle came over, a new worry in his eyes. Gary said, "I'm leaving you in charge here until I come back. Keep them in camp until McCabe gets back."

"Maybe he won't be coming back," Wringle said. "I hear he rode out toward Iron Hand's country. Wasn't that woman you rescued married to his brother or something?"

"News gets around," Gary said curtly, hoping that would end the prying talk.

"How come you're ordered back?" Wringle asked. "Oh, the soldiers talked. Didn't expect them to keep quiet, did you?"

"I guess not," Gary said. "Wringle, if I gave you an order, would you obey it?"

"I guess I would."

"Then get this straight: if I'm not back in two weeks, pack up the camp and come back to Fort Elliot." He went on before anyone could stop him. "I know that's not the way it was supposed to be, but I'm trying to do what's right for you people. McCabe's gone, and I don't know if he'll come back or not. Our friendship with Iron Hand was thin to begin with, and now it's shot down the drain because of the woman I took. The responsibility for this is mine, so you have nothing to worry about. The way I figure it, Iron Hand is just as likely to make a raid on you as not. He sure knows what we're here for. I just don't want anyone killed."

"All right. Two weeks. If you're not back then, we'll pack up and pull out." Wringle turned and walked away to tell the others.

Liam Donovan had the horse saddled and Gary's gear lashed on.

"I'll walk with you," Jane said.

He wanted a moment alone with her, but he was to have only that for Sergeant Goldman was impatient to leave, and the civilians kept gathering around, looking on.

"Some of the orders you get in the army are real stupid," Gary said. "I hate saying good-by, Jane. Especially when I don't know what's over the next hill for any of us. But I'll try to get back."

"Don't if it means doing anything against regulations."

She smiled at him. "You're a very sincere man, Jim, and because of that, somewhat foolish. Remember that we're not worth it. If we were, we could do for ourselves." She bent forward and kissed him lightly. "Was she pretty, the woman you rescued?"

"Yes," he said. "Why do you ask?"

"Lieutenant, we ought to be going!" Goldman called out.

"Yes, yes! In a moment!"

"Jim, I hope you don't come back," Jane said. "Then we'll leave too and we'll never get started again. Believe me, most of us want to give it up, but many of us aren't honest enough to admit it. We made a mistake and it's snowballed into one huge mess. I want to go back to Fort Elliot, to give it up. My brother's dead. Let's bury him and get it over with."

"Lieutenant!"

"All right, Sergeant! Good-by, Jane. I'll see you."

He ran to his horse and stepped into the saddle; Goldman was already turning the detail; they rode north immediately and when Gary looked back, Jane Donovan was standing alone, her arm upraised like some small statue. He waved to her, then did not look back again.

Guthrie McCabe spent a most unpleasant evening, tied to four solidly driven stakes while the children amused themselves until bedtime by lighting small twigs and placing them on his bare stomach.

Iron Hand and his favorite braves watched this, but McCabe robbed them of genuine enjoyment by failing to cry out even once, although he had to bite his lips until they bled. Finally, at Iron Hand's signal, the children were shooed away and McCabe was cut free of the stakes.

"There will be more tomorrow night," Iron Hand said.

"I can hardly wait," McCabe said.

He had momentarily forgotten Iron Hand's knowledge of English and complete lack of a sense of humor; McCabe was seized by the hair and beaten soundly with a coup stick.

"Iron Hand does not think McCabe is a friend. There is no honor in McCabe. Soon, when we are through, he will stop laughing. His eyes will not see the things to laugh at, and he will have no tongue to make sounds. McCabe lies and cheats and brings false friends into Iron Hand's village."

"And Iron Hand is an old woman who will not let me speak," McCabe said. "Iron Hand is thick in the head. He should sing his death song and die, for he is not a leader."

The insult was meant to cut deep, and it did; Iron Hand half rose and raised his hand to strike, then he settled back, his eyes a bright glitter in the firelight. "Why does McCabe return? Does he think Iron Hand will know rest until Stone Calf's killer is dead?"

"Stone Calf was a little boy fit for hunting rabbits. Else he would not have allowed himself to be killed by a white man." McCabe laughed. "Stone Calf should hunt sparrows with a net."

This was worth a kick in the face, and McCabe's head whacked the dirt, then he sat up again. "Tell me where Stone Calf's sons were?" McCabe said. "Did they hide in the rushes when their father rode out to bring back what was never his to take?" McCabe shook his head. "I come alone, Iron Hand, but soon many white men will come and there aren't enough men in your tribe to stop them. Soon all Comanches will join Stone Calf, for Comanches are thieves who steal women and children."

"Enough!" Iron Hand shouted; he was on his feet, stiff with anger. "There will be no quick death for McCabe, the enemy of all Comanches. You will be guarded well, day and night, and you will do a squaw's work until your arms ache and your fingers fall to the ground. Naked you will walk among us, and the children will hurl stones at you and pelt you with sticks and the women will turn their faces from you. You will rise before all others and sleep only after others have gone to rest. Each time you falter you will be beaten, and your food will be the slops left over from the dogs. I have spoken, McCabe. Your days will be long and many numbered, and each day a new death worse than the one before."

"You're a generous son-of-a-bitch," McCabe said, getting to his feet. He bent low at the waist, bowing, and Iron Hand was fascinated by this, thinking it was some part of the white man's ritual. At the proper moment, McCabe uncorked himself, balled his fist, and caught Iron Hand flush on the mouth. The blow sent the Comanche back, knocking down three men behind him; they all ended asprawl. Iron Hand was hastily raised to his feet. His lips were a ruin and seven front teeth were broken; he spat them on the ground.

"Tie him! Beat him!"

The Comanches knew how to do that to perfection. No rawhide for them, just slender willow branches incapable of drawing blood with a single blow, but after two hours, after a thousand blows, McCabe's back was a bleeding mass. He was cut down unconscious and left to lay where he fell. Later that night, while the camp slept, a mangy dog came over to share his warmth.

To waken him in the morning, water was poured over his face and he was driven to his feet like a lazy horse. He had wood to fetch for a dozen fires and everyone wanted his services at once. He made many trips for water, and in a daze, finished out the day, but they kept him working late into the night.

The children were a constant cancer, hitting him, running after him, pelting him with fresh horse manure. He was a man naked in body, and after the fifth day of this, naked in soul.

To live, that was his one thought. To survive and suffer in utter silence, for he was not allowed to speak to anyone; he tried and was beaten for his trouble. The children soon tired of pestering him; there is little pleasure in tormenting someone who can not fight back. He found some relief there, but his work was heavy and constant and he ate off the ground from the scraps thrown to the dogs; he even fought them for the bones with meat still clinging to them.

He thought of Gary often, and of Jane; this helped him

89

to keep going, then he stopped thinking of them altogether. There was no escape for him, he knew, for he was watched constantly by braves who never relaxed their vigil.

Occasionally he saw Iron Hand with his new face and toothless smile, but Iron Hand merely glanced at him and went on his way, leaving McCabe with the feeling that he did not exist at all.

The camp moved unexpectedly on the tenth day, and McCabe carried his load the same as the horses. They walked for two days, then stopped by a creek; McCabe judged that they were another thirty miles south now, thirty miles farther to go if he could break away.

He began to make plans, working carefully so as to establish a routine. Nothing lulled a man like routine; he hoped the guards would grow lax, even for a few minutes. But they did not. The guards were changed often, every day, and Iron Hand seemed to know McCabe's thoughts; his work was changed, breaking the routine, destroying his hopes, his plans.

The thought came slowly to McCabe, as bitter thoughts do, but it was there—the realization that he would never get away.

He would die here.

16

Senator Clifton Tremain took the first train west after receiving Colonel Frazer's wire, and he had sufficient influence with the chairman of the board to have the engineer break a few records. An army detail met him at the railhead and quickly carried him to Fort Elliot. He arrived thirteen hours before Lieutenant Jim Gary, who took his time, rested the horses, and left Sergeant Goldman with the impression that he didn't care whether or not he got to Fort Elliot.

Gary checked in with the officer-of-the-day, then went to his quarters, took a leisurely bath, changed his clothes, and carefully shaved. Only then did he report to Colonel Frazer, who waited impatiently in his office.

The orderly closed the door and Frazer waved him into a chair. "Senator Tremain has been asking me how we were coming along with our prisoner recovery. I told him well. And I hope you substantiate that, Lieutenant Gary."

"We've recovered two prisoners, sir. Janice Tremain and a boy, in his early teens. Unfortunately the boy killed a female member of the camp and was hung."

Frazer dropped his cigar. "He was what?"

"Hung, sir. A fit of frenzy, I'm afraid, but by the time they cooled down, he was dead. Actually, he had it coming and I don't think they were really sorry about their part in it."

Colonel Frazer sat down weakly and wiped a shaking hand across his face. "In the name of heaven, do you calmly sit there and tell me that after all this time you have recovered only two prisoners, and that one was killed? What have you been doing out there, Gary? Picking flowers?"

"No, sir. We've been quite busy, sir."

"The officer-of-the-day reports to me that several wagons came back from Sand Creek. He's checking on the particulars."

"I believe they're discouraged, sir," Gary said. "May I ask why I was recalled to the post?"

"Why, because Senator Tremain wants to talk to you. What did you think?" Frazer shook his head as though he were dealing with an idiot and did not want to lose his patience. "This evening, the senator is giving a party for the officers and their wives in honor of his niece's return." He glanced at his watch. "That will give you exactly two hours and fourteen minutes to have your written report finished and on my desk. That will be all, Gary."

"Yes, sir."

He went outside, and on the porch he pursed his lips for a silent whistle. If Frazer was shocked now, Gary could only imagine what he would feel when the report reached his desk. The score: two captives returned, one now deceased. Iron Hand antagonized. His brother, Stone Calf, killed. Guthrie McCabe missing, assuredly a prisoner of the Comanches, possibly dead. General morale of the civilians, very low. Six per cent returning to Fort Elliot. Possibility of that growing to 25 per cent most likely. Future prospects of recovery, very slight. Total abandonment suggested.

With the report on Frazer's desk, Gary walked to the officer's mess, now gayly lighted and brightly decorated for the dance. The musicians were there, tuning their small band and two orderlies scattered soap chips over the floor.

One man stood alone, tall, pleasantly featured, somewhere in his early sixties; he seemed to be waiting for Gary, for he took his arm as soon as he stepped inside.

"You are Gary, aren't you? Good! I'm Clifton Tremain." He guided Gary to the punch bowl, speaking quite confidentially. Tremain was a likable man, soft-spoken, friendly; he gave Gary the impression that he had spent his life doing favors for other people and did not regret any of them. "I've been wanting to meet you, Lieutenant. And please try this punch. I understand that mixed among the neuter fruit juices there swirls two quarts of the sutler's best whisky." He laughed and dippered a glass for Gary.

He offered a silent toast, then drank some of the punch. A frown momentarily made a furrowed field of his forehead. "Ah, I may be mistaken there, Mr. Gary. Perhaps it is closer to three quarts, and not the sutler's best. Does that taste like horse linament to you? No matter. I'm glad you came early. We have some matters to discuss."

"Exactly what, sir?"

"There's a matter of a reward, Mr. Gary. Janice is my brother's daughter. Surely you did not expect to go unrewar—" He stopped talking as Gary's expression froze slightly. "Of course! That was damned stupid of me, Gary. You'll have to forgive me. I'm so used to dealing with favor seekers and putting my hand on my bankroll when a favor is done." He put his hand on Gary's shoulder and gave him a shake. "You're a gentleman. Forgive me for forgetting it."

"That's all right, sir."

"I wish everything else was all right." He steered Gary to some seats along the wall, where they could talk quietly, and in private. "Janice has said very little to me about her life in captivity. I thought perhaps, since you delivered her, she confided more in you. Understand me, Gary. I want to help her."

"She must understand that, Senator. If you give her a little more time——"

"No, no, I'm not making myself clear. Gary, the people who live here, the officers and their wives, they understand what it is to be a prisoner of the Comanches. Now Janice is returned safely. True, she has been worked hard, but that's all. Talk is one thing, but speculation is another. What people think is often more important than what they say." He took out his handkerchief and wiped his face; he was perspiring somewhat. "Gary, this isn't easy for me, to talk like this, but I must talk to someone. I thought you'd be the logical one." He paused to light a cigar. "Like I say, Janice has remained silent about her years as a prisoner. That can be worse than the truth at times. The wives on this post talk, Gary, and you know how that goes. They operate on the theory that if you have nothing to hide, you'll speak. So Janice must be guilty of—of anything you want to imagine. I'm giving this dance in her honor, Gary. I thought it would be a fitting homecoming. Perhaps I was wrong. Oh, I'm sure the attendance will be what it should be. Frazer doesn't want to offend me and his officers don't want to offend him. But I'm afraid there are more ways than one to hurt someone. Gary, in Washington, I've seen politics at its worst. You can kill a person by looking through them, talking around them, ignoring them. I don't want that to happen to Janice."

"Yes, sir. I understand. Senator, I know the officers on this post and I don't think it will be like that at all."

"Do you know their wives?"

"I'm afraid I don't understand, sir."

"Do you know their wives? Or how any woman squeezes a man? Just let a husband cross his wife the wrong way and the food gets bad and his fun gets cut off at the pockets." He frowned. "Politics is better than this, Gary, believe me. At least you know what to expect there, and past experience has taught you all the dirty tricks."

"Senator, I can assure you——"

"I'm too old a man to be assured anymore," Tremain said. "Frankly, I believe in what I pay for, and am willing to insult you again by offering you a handsome remuneration to see that Janice is not deserted."

Color stained Gary's cheeks, and he got up slowly. "Senator, it could be that I fully intended to do just that, because I wanted to, or for my own reasons. But now you've changed

93

all that. Whatever I do now will be spoiled. Spoiled because you've put a price on it."

"I haven't yet," Tremain said. "I thought I'd let you do that."

"Do we really have anything more to say to each other, sir?"

"No, I guess not," Tremain said. "Gary, was she an Indian's—well, were there any children anywhere?"

"Good-night, sir," Gary said stiffly and left the hall. He let the first coolness of night fan away his anger, and then he walked slowly to the infirmary; guests were always billeted there. He could not hate Tremain, who was nagged by the same fears as other men. He could not blame him because he too had wished that she was different; he was a prudish man who wanted all women pure, until they were married at least. And that meant being married to him, not some other man first.

Gary felt slightly ashamed because he had blamed Tremain; he felt as Tremain did, so he had no right to be indignant, no right to be righteous. He had condemned her himself, and this bothered him.

She answered the door and was surprised to see him. Stepping aside, she ushered him inside, then closed the door. Gone were the cast-off Indian trappings; she wore a pale rose dress with a tight waist and collar and a puff of ruffles around her wrists. Her hair was clean and shining; she wore a ribbon in it, which made her seem young and frightfully innocent.

"Someone told me Uncle Clifton sent for you," Janice said. "It seems that someone is always sending for someone, or doing something that someone else doesn't want. Won't you sit down?"

"Thank you."

"Smoke if you like." She found a saucer for the cigar ashes, then took the other chair across from him. "This is the first time I've ever seen you without dirt on your face and you're quite handsome. What happened to your head?"

"I fell up a tree."

She smiled. "I see. Mind my own business."

"No, it isn't like that. Really, it's not worth explaining." He put a match to his cigar, then blew smoke toward the ceiling. "The party tonight was a stupid idea. He ought to have taken you home. But I guess he's human, he's got to try to make up for the lost years."

"I'm glad you came to see me, Jim. Glad because you know about me which saves a lot of painful explanation. That's

94

a very selfish reason, isn't it? But I think you understand."

"Made any plans?"

"No, and I don't want to. Do you have the time?"

He took out his pocket watch and consulted it. "A quarter to eight."

"I suppose it would be inconsiderate to keep them waiting, wouldn't it?" She took her wrap off the bed and flung it over her shoulders. "Will you walk with me, Jim?"

"Yes, it would be a pleasure." He opened the door for her, then closed it after him. She waited at the base of the steps and he offered her his arm; together they crossed the dark parade, listening to the music grow louder; the dance had already begun. At the doorway, Janice paused, took a deep breath, then stepped inside, her hand resting lightly on Gary's arm.

Whether by design or chance, the music ended and couples stood on the floor, politely clapping, all eyes turned to Janice Tremain. These army functions were not new to Gary, and normally a few men would have approached and asked her to dance. At least the single men would have, and there were nine, not counting himself, at Fort Elliot. Yet they remained in their clannish knot by the punch bowl, and by their stillness, drew attention to her. Gary expected the married men to mind their wives, but not the bachelors.

The music began again, and there was that awful moment when she stood there, trying to keep her composure from breaking, while the genteel of Fort Elliot moved in their own exclusive circle. The anger returned to Gary, but he kept it out of his voice when he spoke.

"Will you do me the honor? I dance most awkwardly though."

She put a bright, superficial smile on her face, leaving the hurt unerased from her eyes. "I think that is a lie," she said and lifted her arms.

He was not as awkward as he claimed, and he danced carefully because it had been years since she had heard anything but chanting and he did not want her to trip, embarrass her further. She was a tense branch in his arms, but in a moment she began to relax. She smiled at him again and said, "See? It was a lie. You dance well."

"Don't speak too soon. If I step on your feet, I'll trip on the hem of your dress. Did I tell you that I took dancing lessons when I was nine? It's a fact. One lesson and I was expelled forever."

The dance ended too quickly for both of them and they stood undecided for a moment. Dancing, there was an excuse for their being together, but now that the dance had ended, Gary understood that no one would approach her, and he would have to dance with her again, and again, which made her as much a leper as if no one had danced with her at all.

He led her to the punch bowl and handed her a full glass. Senator Tremain eased over to them and helped himself. His face was stiffly set and he spoke to Gary. "Everyone's thirst seems to have vanished."

"I'm poisoning the water hole," Janice said softly.

"Nonsense!" Tremain said sharply, because it was true and he resented it. "Janice, I wanted this to be fun for you."

She looked at him oddly. "Fun? Uncle, how could it possibly be fun? And don't blame them. Blame me, for being here."

"Now let's not talk like that," Tremain snapped. "Gary, what kind of friends do you have here? Frazer will hear of this rudeness, you can bet on it."

"Please," she said. "The solution is quite simple." She put her punch glass aside and looked around the room. The small talk faded as though they waited for her to speak.

"Don't do anything dumb," Jim Gary warned.

"I'll do what I have to do." She folded her hands together in front of her. "Ladies. And gentlemen." She put just the right inflection on the gentlemen, a light lifting of tone, which was enough, for they knew what they were and scarcely needed reminding of it. "I want to thank you for appearing here this evening. It was in effect, a command performance, but my uncle meant well. Since I was released, since I returned here, I've said very little to any of you. Perhaps you think I've rejected your offers of friendship. I didn't mean to, and for my rudeness, I must apologize."

"Janice!" Gary whispered, but she shook her head slightly, silencing him.

"All of you know that I was a prisoner of the Comanches. There may be one or two among you who know first-hand what that is like. To those who do not, I'll not keep you wondering any longer. After a year and a half, I was taken for a wife by Stone Calf, who was a brother to Iron Hand. In his way, he was a good man, who beat me only when I deserved it, and who killed his enemies quickly, with honor. We had no children, which I often regret; I think it would have made life more tolerable for me. Certainly it was, in any event, more tolerable than my position here. Now, enjoy yourselves. Jim, will you walk with me to my quarters?"

"Yes," he said. Then he looked across the room to the

junior officers. "Calvin, Upston, and you, O'Flynn, I'll see you behind the rifle butts at dawn."

"Aw, Jim," one began, then closed his mouth.

He took Janice Tremain's arm and walked her outside. Shielded by the dark coolness of the porch, she stopped and leaned against the upright. The wind blew on her face and she closed her eyes tightly. "That was hard, Jim. Harder to do than anything I've ever done."

"You were magnificent, Janice."

Senator Tremain stepped to the door, intending to come out, and Jim Gary motioned him back. He hesitated as though it was difficult to obey someone else, then he turned and went back inside.

"I'm all right now," Janice said.

"Are you sure?"

She looked at him quickly, then she smiled and he saw that her fear, her tension had vanished. "Yes, I'm very sure. Everything will be all right now."

17

Colonel Frazer was in a towering rage. He paced back and forth in his office and occasionally glared at the four officers standing poker stiff, their eyes locked front and center. Lieutenant Gary had a swollen upper lip and one eye was discolored and puffed. The three other officers bore more vivid marks and Lieutenant O'Flynn's breath bubbled through the smashed cartilage of his nose.

"Utterly disgraceful!" Frazer roared. "Fighting!" He wheeled about and faced Gary. "What do you intend to do, Lieutenant Gary? Trounce every bachelor on the post?"

"Yes, sir. There's Muldoon, Riggs, Cunningham, Shea, Parkinson and Dulop left, sir."

Frazer shook his finger inches from Gary's nose. "If I hear of you ever going near the rifle butts again, I'll have you court-martialed!" He waved his arms like a young bird trying to fly. "Now clear out of here. And have the contract surgeon take a look at you."

They saluted and did an about-face, Academy perfect.

"Not you, Gary! The rest of you may go."

When the door closed, Frazer gave Gary the order to about-face again, but left him standing at attention. "Lieutenant Gary, with unbelieving eyes I read your report, not once, but five times. You have failed miserably, sir! Miserably."

"Yes, sir. I believe McCabe warned you of that possibility——"

"God damn McCabe! I don't want to hear his name mentioned!" He sat down behind his desk and drummed his fingers. "Gary, do you understand that I have but little time left? You act as though I were going to be in the army for another ten years, that I have the time to smooth out your incompetent mistakes."

"No, sir."

"I send you on a routine task, difficult to be sure, but not impossible, and you bungle it. Gary, you're not putting your heart into your duty, and I'll so note it on your record. That captaincy is flying out the window, or don't you care about that?"

"Yes, sir." He licked his lips. "Colonel, I think it's a mistake to go further with this. I noted that in my report and——"

"I read the damned thing! Get it through your head that we can not abandon this. Why, Washington would make a shambles of the army. Where do you think our appropriations come from? Heaven? Taxpayers have spoken, Gary, and now we jump. I've talked to Senator Tremain about this, and he endorses my view completely. Now I want an accurate appraisal of our possibilities. We have no choice but to continue."

Gary thought of changing that a little, for it was Frazer who wouldn't accept the choice of passing this on to his successor and not making brigadier on retirement. But a junior officer has to keep his mouth closed; Gary was in enough trouble as it was.

"Well, sir, I think a peaceful negotiation with Iron Hand is out of the question. Besides, the civilians are ready to drop this and go——"

Frazer waved his hands. "I'm not concerned now with what they want or what's good for them. They set the wheels in motion and now it's too late for them to change their minds."

"We just run over them, eh, sir?"

"If it has to be done," Frazer said. "So discount the possibility of my dropping this. I won't have the last notation on my record read that I failed to complete an assignment, or have my successor finish it for me. No, Lieutenant Gary, I believe this calls for a punitive expedition."

"I beg your pardon, sir?"

"A hundred men," Frazer said. "Yes, that ought to be enough. We'll have to be careful though in order not to violate the terms of the treaty."

"An armed movement would——"

"Unarmed, except for pistols and sabers," Frazer said. "Does this not pique your fancy, Lieutenant? You can make your base at Sand Creek with the civilians and make your sallies from there. If I read the treaty correctly, and I assure you that I do, I am within my rights to take troops into Iron Hand's country on matters involving the government. Now McCabe is a government scout and he is being held prisoner, or at worst, killed. Either way it's no great loss to Texas, but a blessing to me because this puts Iron Hand in direct treaty violation. Naturally the entire area will have to be combed, and all white prisoners taken. It will be easy to say that they will have to be brought here for identification, and turned loose if they are not McCabe. Of course they will be given over to their rightful relatives and we can appease Iron Hand and his sub-chiefs later with an extra beef ration."

For a moment, Lieutenant Gary was too appalled to speak. Finally he said, "And what if the Comanches resist?"

"It will be part of your duty to see that there is no trouble."

"Mine, sir?"

"Of course. You'll command the detail. At this moment I consider you most expendable. I'll give you Shea and Riggs; their careers are as yet unestablished and disgrace is always less important to men of twenty-three than of sixty. Providing, of course, that you bobble this badly. Succeed, and you're a captain."

"Colonel, I could resign my commission."

"We all can, but we never do."

"Yes," Gary said. "You've got a point there. When am I expected to depart with this expedition, sir?"

Frazer paused. "With rations to draw, stock to select, men to pick, I believe a week or ten days would be reasonable."

"Very good, sir. I expect the Sand Creek camp will be vacant by then anyway."

"What's that?"

"Before I left, sir, I gave orders for them to vacate the camp if I didn't return within a specified time. There's no need for them to remain there, with myself and McCabe gone."

"That was quite a responsibility to assume," Frazer said. "However, it's just as well, the way it's working out. That will be all, Lieutenant Gary. I'd get busy in the morning, if I were you. Shea and Riggs will be notified."

Gary saluted and left the office.

He supposed that he ought to go over to the infirmary and talk to Janice Tremain, but he held himself back. There was no sense in talking with her just for the sake of talk; she needed a man who meant what he said, whose interest in her was genuine because she was a desirable woman. And Gary didn't feel that way. He wished he could, but he could not. She needed the kind of a man who could ignore the looks, the talk that would forever follow her. Or perhaps a man big enough to lift her above this, lift her so high that no one would ever dare to speak of those five years.

And I'm not that kind of a man, Gary thought. He wanted to be, but wanting it wasn't enough. She needed a man like McCabe who could be as hard toward the world as it was toward him. That's not me, Gary thought. I'm jelly inside, and McCabe's gone now. He felt sorry for Janice Tremain, and a little sorry for himself.

18

The Indian agent made a special trip from Fort Dodge to put his reluctant endorsement on Colonel Frazer's punitive expedition; the agent recognized the legal validity of Frazer's move, but questioned the wisdom of his judgment. However, he affixed his signature to the document that made legal the movement of troops in Comanche country, then took the first stage back to Dodge, as if by leaving the fort he could forget this was happening, or be blamed less for his part in it.

Lieutenant Gary worked his force into shape, carefully selecting men and mounts and seeing that all rations, forage, and equipment were ready. He worked slowly, carefully, as though in fear of making a mistake, while in reality he wanted to give the civilians at Sand Creek plenty of time to depart and return to Fort Elliot. By his figuring, they were already on the move, so he asked Colonel Frazer for permission to quit the post four days early. This was a sound move, for Frazer interpreted it as eagerness and erased some of his harsher thoughts concerning Lieutenant Gary.

With his command behind him, Lieutenant Gary had fourteen miles beneath him when the sunrise was full and a new heat began to grow over the land. Divided into three sections, Gary rode at the head of the column of twos, scouts out, flankers to the left and right, and Lieutenants Shea and Riggs eating dust at the center and drag.

He held the march to regulations, saving men and horses, and camped that first night in the open. Some miles beyond —he did not know how many—the civilian wagons would be camping, and he considered the wisdom of sending a rider ahead to contact them. Then he decided that the meeting should appear to be chance, and rolled into his blankets.

Command kept him busy; he had a hundred things to check, for a good commander knows what goes on in his troop. Gary was the last to mount and he waved them southward, pushing across the first dawn light and the miles of emptiness ahead.

In the middle of the afternoon, the scout reported dust to the left and Gary altered course, contacting the first wagon two hours later. He gave orders to camp and as soon as the squad fires were lighted and the picket lines established, he turned over the detail to Shea and walked across the five-hundred yard interval to the first wagon, thinking it was Wringle's.

Sean Donovan met him, shook hands briefly, then said, "Jane's visitin' the Pardeen wagon, Lieutenant."

"Where's Wringle?"

"Sand Creek. He said he was going to stay and I guess he meant it." Donovan reached into the wagon and brought out a jug. "I like a little snort at evenin' time. Join me?"

"Sure," Gary said and laid it in the crook of his arm. He sighed and handed it back and wiped tears from his eyes. "That paint remover?"

"No, but it'll do the job. Where you going with the soldiers?"

"The colonel wants the job done," Gary said. He turned when he heard Jane's step. She ran to him and he believed she would have kissed him if her father had not been there.

"Jim, I'm glad to see you. We left too early, didn't we?"

"No, you left just in time."

"Stay for supper," she invited.

"I should be with my men. Well, I guess it'll be all right."

"What kind of a job does the colonel want done?" Sean Donovan asked.

"He wants us to take all the white captives from the Comanches, without force, if possible."

"Is it possible?" Jane asked.

Jim Gary shrugged. "Maybe. But likely it isn't. McCabe didn't come back?"

They both shook their heads.

"Well, I didn't think he would," Gary said. "And this time it isn't because he doesn't want to. One of the main reasons I'm going along with Frazer is to see if I can find McCabe."

"Or where they buried him," Sean Donovan said.

"Jim, didn't you explain to the colonel that we're going home, that we've had enough? We've given up again, but this time it's for good. If any of our kin is alive, we don't want to know about it. We just want to forget now."

"Too late for that," Gary said. "He said that this will have to be finished to clean the record. I only follow orders, Jane. Some of them, like this one, I don't like, but I follow just the same."

"You planning to take those you rescue back to Fort Elliot?" Sean asked.

"That's the order."

"He don't know what he's doing," Sean Donovan said. "He just don't know at all." He walked away, sadly shaking his head.

"Sit down," Jane said. "I have to make supper." She opened

the chest that held her cooking pots, then rummaged through the food chest. "Beans and hoecake and pork again. I'm getting pretty tired of that."

"When I get back," Gary said, "I'll take you to Tascosa and buy you the best meal in town. Then we'll go to the opera house and see the show."

"I'll hold you to that," she said. He watched her make the batter for the cake, and cut the pork into thick slices, and put the pot of beans on to boil. Without looking up from her work, she asked, "Did you see her at Fort Elliot, Jim?"

"Janice Tremain?"

"Is that her name? I didn't know it."

"Yes, I saw her," Gary said. "An uncle of hers came from back East to get her. Now he wishes he'd stayed home." He told her about the dance and Jane Donovan watched him carefully as he talked. The sun was dropping, shooting out a last slant of light, then the shades of gray started to grow deeper. "So she had it against her if she kept silent or spoke out," Gary said. "But I guess it helped her to speak."

"I think I would have kept silent," Jane said softly. "It's bad enough to know of the wrong in you, but I think it's worse when everyone else knows it too."

"There's no wrong in you, Jane."

"Jim, there's wrong in all of us." She covered the pot of beans and put the frying pan on to heat.

He got up. "I really should return to my men, but I'll be back for supper."

He walked slowly to the command post, a tent erected near the center of the compound. Lieutenant Shea was polishing his boots when Gary sat down.

When the sergeant came by, Gary left word that the troop would be fed and ready to ride by dawn; he meant to move on without delay, without saying anything to Jane Donovan.

The trouble with me, Gary told himself, was that he did most everything because he felt sorry for someone; he would have to quit that habit before it got him into something serious. He admitted that he had rescued Janice Tremain for that reason, and almost ruined his military career by speaking critically of Frazer's decision, just because he knew that the civilians had had enough and he was sorry for them. And now he was adding it up and silently crying in his beer because he felt sorry for himself.

This is one hell of a mess, Gary thought.

By noon they were deep in Iron Hand's country, and Jim Gary was not so naïve as to assume that they were unobserved. A hundred-man column raises considerable dust, and noise, regardless of the care exercised to do otherwise, so he assumed that Indian runners were already scurrying ahead with the word that the long knives were marching.

That afternoon he found the first of the camps, deserted of course, but a broad trail led away and he followed it, giving up the idea of scouting out other lesser camps. They were moving, lodges, women and all, toward the main camp, under Iron Hand's wing, so he would meet them there, fell them if he had to with one bold stroke.

A very gallant thought, he knew, but hardly likely to turn out that way. Iron Hand would gird himself for war, and Gary wondered how he could prevent it; he knew he could not handle war with a hundred men, not armed with pistols and sabers. Maybe that's what Frazer had figured; he'd retire in a burst of glory, singing praises of the dead officers and men slaughtered by the warlike Comanches. Another Custer episode.

He did not expect Iron Hand to move his camp now; likely he would deploy his braves and meet Gary somewhere between. Or he might leave only the women, children, and captives in the camp, tended by old men—that was a common trick. Gary could then have his unopposed way, but in trying to ride out, he would find himself surrounded.

Iron Hand, in spite of his paint, was a soldier, a tactician; he had chosen for his campsite, a depression of land surrounded by three prominent ridges, and Gary topped one of these late in the afternoon, drawing his column to a halt.

His hand motion brought Lieutenant Shea forward from the second section and together they looked upon the camp. Women moved about, doing their never-ending work, and the children played, only closer to their lodges than usual, and here and there an old man crouched down with his blanket and solitary thoughts. The smoke from the lodge fires rose sluggishly in the still air, and the camp seemed normal, to the casual eye.

But Gary knew that every brave of warring age was gone, probably in a position to attack them at the first hostile move.

"Now what?" Shea asked.

"Draw them in one line abreast," Gary said. "I want a line of mounted blue on this ridge. Pistols and sabers at the raised position, and I'll court-martial the first man who lowers them." Shea frowned and Gary ignored his disapproval. He motioned toward the camp. "See those lodges on the out fringes? They haven't been there very long. Iron Hand's camp is twice the size it was when I was last in it. All the sub-chiefs within fifty miles have moved in on him for protection."

104

"Protection from what? Pistols and sabers?" He nodded toward the hollow. "Before we get halfway down there, Iron Hand will cut us to ribbons." His eyes raised to the other ridges. "There's a Comanche with a rifle behind every depression."

"More like two," Gary said calmly. "Would you send Sergeants Davis and Ellsworth forward, please?"

"Yes, sir." Shea wheeled and Gary waited there until the two enlisted men came forward. Shea and Riggs returned with them, but waited in the background, just within hearing distance.

"Gentlemen, I'm picking you to volunteer to go into that camp with me. Select ten privates apiece, and bring them along."

"Volunteers, sir?" Davis asked.

Gary looked at him and smiled thinly. "Davis, they're always volunteers, aren't they?"

"Yes, sir. Come on, Ellsworth."

When they rode back to pick the men, Gary watched the line form, a very long line, properly dressed, with each man holding his weapons raised.

Shea could stand this no longer. He edged up and said, "Gary, you'll never get away with this."

"It is a gamble, isn't it?" Then the sergeants returned with the men and Gary led them at a walk off the ridge.

19

Although the women and children did not scatter when Gary rode into the village, he saw that they were badly frightened, but not too frightened for their men were nearby, waiting for some signal before attacking. Halting his detail before Iron Hand's lodge, Gary said, "Sergeant Ellsworth, take ten men and scour the village. Take into protective custody any white person, male or female, regardless of age. You take the remaining men and do the same, Davis."

"Yes, sir." They formed their groups and turned to ride away, each starting at the far end of the village. Hardly had they begun to move when Ellsworth said, "Whoops," and pointed to the south ridge.

Even in this moment of acute danger, Jim Gary thought it was an impressive sight, awesome. And if he lived, he would always remember vividly this moment when half a thousand half-naked men looked down on him with pointed rifles. His heart hammered and his face felt feverish, yet he enjoyed the moment immensely, for this was the test of which a man dreams, when his courage is supremely tested and he finds himself strong.

"Hold up!" Gary said. He cupped his hands around his mouth. "With so many braves at his back, is Iron Hand afraid to meet me?"

He could not distinguish the leader, not until a lone Comanche detached himself from the others and came down the slope, the sun glinting from the polished hook that was his hand. Gary rode to meet him halfway, then stopped.

Iron Hand was painted for war and he spoke curtly. "Does the enemy of Iron Hand wish to be destroyed?"

"Must we speak of war? I came to speak of peace."

"With soldiers?" He waved toward Gary's force. "There can be no peace."

"The white soldier chief wants the prisoners of the Comanches," Gary said. "The one called McCabe is the property of the white soldier chief."

"McCabe is mine. He works with the women and sleeps with the dogs. No one takes what is Iron Hand's."

"I mean to take him, because those are my orders. But I want to take him in peace."

"No peace. You turn back or die."

"Look to my hill, Iron Hand. How many soldiers will die?"

"Half," Iron Hand said.

"And the other half will enter your village and kill the women and children. Then you will have an empty victory, Iron Hand. In ten years, there will be no more Comanches on this earth. Men will forget your name. The dust will cover the tracks you have made, and all will be dead."

"All white soldiers will die!"

"Yes, but the Comanches will die with them," Gary said. "Without women, the Comanche is dead, even if we cannot kill many today." He gave Iron Hand a moment to consider this before speaking again. "There will be no more beef issue from the white soldier chief. The Comanche will hunt like a dog for scraps to eat. That is what war will bring if Iron Hand wants it. Make up your mind, Iron Hand. Today is the day when all Comanches begin a slow death." He decided to give this one more push. "Which is more important to Iron Hand? Keeping the white slaves he has and dying forever? Or giving them up and living to old age?"

He was an intelligent man without grace and he made one final disgusted motion with his hand, then threw his rifle into the dirt. From the Comanche line a wail went up, but it was over, and Gary spoke quietly to his sergeants.

"Get on with it now. We don't want to waste time here."

He waited with Iron Hand while the miserable, painful business was done. From the warriors, young white boys were taken, physically bound, for they fought wildly, and were escorted to the hill where the line of blue waited. Women were herded together, some carrying their small children in their arms, the older ones following dutifully.

Comanche braves remained wooden faced as their "wives" and children were gathered, and crying ran through the camp, for none seemed eager to be returned. Sergeant Davis found Guthrie McCabe, and gave him a blanket with which to cover his nakedness, then brought him to where Gary waited, his expression impassive.

McCabe was thirty pounds lighter, bearded, dirty, and too stunned to be grateful. He kept scratching the vermin that pestered him continually, and moving his bare feet around in the dust as though he wanted to run and forced himself not to.

The prisoners were like cattle being driven, and they kept turning their heads and calling out to husbands and fathers and so much emotion gripped Comanche and white alike that Gary grew fearful that Iron Hand might not be able to hold back his braves. A few broke and ran to the gathering and tried to embrace a wife or a child, only to be driven back by the soldiers.

107

Even when they were on the ridge with the soldiers, Jim Gary could hear the wailing. A ring of mounted men rode around them to keep them from breaking away, then Gary had had enough; his business here was at a sickening end.

"Mount behind me," he told McCabe, then helped the man onto the horse. Quickly he rode up the flank of the ridge, organized his command, and began the march out.

Shea was in charge of the released prisoners and the only way he could move them was to tie their hands together and put them on a long lead rope. Three miles of this proved that it wouldn't work, for they hung back and slowed the column. Shea then put loops of rope around their necks so that hanging back meant choking. The men gave no trouble, but the women, especially the younger girls, seemed to prefer strangulation to delivery. He had to tie a few to horses, forcing some of the soldiers to ride double.

In this fashion they began the night march, not stopping until midnight, when Gary ordered a camp made near a small creek. A close guard was placed around the rescued, and Gary thought this a strange thing; he could not accustom himself to the idea of such a sudden uprooting.

McCabe was given some clothes, spare shirt and pants, all ill-fitting. He borrowed soap and razor and when he appeared at Gary's fire, he was shaved and bathed. During the ride, he had said nothing, and now the silent mood still clung to him.

"Help yourself to the coffee," Gary said, pouring him a cup.

McCabe hunkered down and drank. Then he said, "All the time they had me, I kept dreaming of a cup of coffee. Now that I'm able to drink it, I find it tastes like mule pee." He looked at Gary for a long moment. "You saved my life, Jim. I wouldn't have lasted out the winter."

"Well, don't thank me for it," Gary said. "The hand heal up?"

McCabe nodded. "I guess the Lord took a look at what was happening to the rest of me and felt sorry. Gary, you saved my life."

"You're repeating yourself, Guthrie."

"I guess I am." He shook his head from side to side. "All my life I've tried not to owe anything to any man, but I sure owe you, Jim."

"You want to square it?"

"Sure," McCabe said.

"Then stand up."

"What?" He frowned. "What for, Jim?"

"So I can know your block off," Gary said.

Guthrie McCabe's frown deepened. "Jim, you're not mad at me, are you? I didn't think you were. What is it then?" He turned his head and looked at the lumped misery being driven back to the arms of their relatives. "You got a mad on against something too big to hit out at, is that it? And you want to pound awhile on McCabe, is that it?" McCabe put his coffee cup aside, then stood up. "All right, Jim. You go ahead and start pounding. I've got a few things to work off myself."

Gary sent his coffee cup flying and launched his attack against McCabe. Their meeting wrung a grunt from both of them, and they faced each other, eyes locked in the sockets, raining fists against flesh. When they parted, both men were bleeding and the sound of the fight drew Shea and Riggs on the run; they stopped just outside the firelight and stared.

Riggs said, "For God's sake, sir! Back away! Back away!"

But there was no backing away in these men, no give at all. They hammered each other and wrestled, flinging each other down, twisting arms, striking out with their knees; they were like wild birds thrashing in the dust, slashing, gouging.

Riggs tried to pull them apart and they turned on him with a raw resentment and beat him to the ground with devastating suddenness; Shea pulled the dazed and bleeding Riggs to safety.

Unable to stand, Gary and McCabe rested on their knees, still throwing punches, then McCabe could take no more of it and he fell on his face. Jim Gary stared at him for a moment, then weakly lay across him, his breathing strained and painful sounding.

Almost timidly, Shea stepped up to him. "Sir? Are you all right, sir?"

Sergeant Ellsworth, whose seventeen years in the army had taught him much, stepped up to the fire. "Leave them alone, sir. They're all right."

Shea was indignant. "What do you mean, all right? They've beat each other to a pulp!"

"Yes, sir. But they're all right, Lieutenant."

"This is damned ridiculous," Shea said and walked away.

The sergeant tried to help Riggs, but was shaken off. Riggs looked at McCabe and Gary. "They ought to be locked up for their own good."

"Yes, sir," Ellsworth said and waited until he left. Then he took a bucket of water and carried it over to Gary, setting it within reach. He too went back to his own fire and waited.

Gary found the bucket and washed his face, flinching when he touched the raw and bleeding areas. Finally he gained his feet, then threw some water over McCabe, who groaned and stirred.

When he could sit up, Gary threw McCabe a towel he had soaked in the water; McCabe washed his face.

"Good fight, huh, Jim?"

"Yes," Gary said. "The best I've had."

"How do you feel?"

"Fine. You?"

"Never better," McCabe said. He looked at Gary and grinned and blood ran down his chin from his smashed lips. "Feel like taking this?" He held out his hand.

Gary took it and they shook solemnly, then McCabe eased himself erect, taking care to protect a new rash of bruises. "That coffee will taste like coffee now, Jim."

"Good thing we didn't kick the pot over." He rummaged around and found the cups; he knocked the dirt out of them, wiped them on his tattered shirttail, then filled both of them.

"Too bad Janice Tremain couldn't have licked someone. Or even got licked. It doesn't matter who wins, does it, Jim?"

"No. Who won this one?"

"I guess I passed out first," McCabe said, smiling. "But I don't care about that." He drank some of his coffee and burned his lips. "What we ought to have done, Jim, is to have roped off a section at Sand Creek and made all those civilians pound each other until all the anger and shame and resentment was gone. They'd have gone home then and there."

"Sure," Gary said. He studied the fire for a time. "I think I'll resign my commission anyway, Guthrie. This is as bad as Chivington's massacre, only we're not doing those women and children the favor of killing them off."

"Be a mess at Fort Elliot," McCabe agreed. "A mess I wish I was well out of." He sighed and drank some more coffee. "You been to Sand Creek lately?"

"No. Why?"

He shrugged. "No reason, I guess, except that four days ago, nine bucks left Iron Hand's village and came back with hair."

Gary's attention sharpened. "You feel like riding, Guthrie?"

"I guess it won't kill me."

"Sergeant!" Gary waited until he came up. "Sergeant, saddle two horses. McCabe and I are leaving. And send Lieutenant Shea here on the double."

"Yes, sir. Sir, we don't have any remuda."

"Then have two light troopers ride double. Just bring McCabe a good horse."

"Yes, sir."

The two men waited in silence until Shea came over to the fire; he viewed both men with open suspicion. "You sent for me, sir?"

"You're in command, Shea. McCabe and I are going to ride over to Sand Creek. Be on the move at dawn and make it twelve hours before your next camp. We'll pick you up around noon, day after tomorrow."

"Yes, sir."

McCabe and Gary were impatient; they walked to the picket line and talked in low tones while their mounts were being saddled. Gary was saying, "Wringle and his wife stayed at Sand Creek after the others left. I was recalled to Fort Elliot for nearly ten days, but I left orders for the civilians to vacate the creek camp. They did. I met them on the way to Iron Hand's village, and they told me that Wringle stayed on."

"That's not good," McCabe said. "Man, being alone out here is just asking for it unless you know what you're doing, and Wringle didn't know anything." He looked toward the horses. "Can't you move any faster over there?"

"Yes, sir. Just be a minute."

"Guthrie, you were there in the village. What did you see?"

"Not much. They kept me working all the time. But I heard talk. Iron Hand's braves brought back hair because there was dancing in Stone Calf's lodge."

Their horses were ready and both men mounted, turning out of the camp immediately. They rode for an hour without speaking, then dismounted to walk the horses; they had a long way to go and had to spare the mounts.

"I'll give you odds Wringle's dead," McCabe said.

"You'll get no takers."

"You've got to see him, huh? I mean, this will go in your damned report, won't it?"

"You know what I'll have to do," Gary said. "Hell, do you think I like the implications? Nobody wants another war with the Comanches, but if it's started, what can you do about it?"

"I know what I'd do."

"Yeah, but you're not army," Gary said. "I am."

20

No morbid sense drove Gary into making an all night ride of it, just a clinical detachment, a positive suspicion that the Wringles were dead. There was a slim, off-chance that he was wrong in his guess, but he did not believe so. Still he had to go to Sand Creek and check for himself, and perhaps bury them, if there was anything left to bury.

He came onto the grove just after dawn, and stopped, trying to find some sign of life. The civilians had left their untidy scars on the land, blackened circles where their cook fires had been, and outhouse pits, and rubbish heaps, for they were people who were always discarding something. Wringle had started to build on the other side of the grove and Gary rode there, McCabe trailing him a few paces behind.

Wringle's wagon, when they came upon it, had been burned for the ironwork it contained, and the two walls were a tumble of logs, also fire-charred.

"Hold up," McCabe said and got down off the horse. He walked forward and from beneath a pile of rubble, lifted the hem of Mrs. Wringle's dress. McCabe then kicked and tore at the rubble until she was uncovered. Her death had been heroic and merciful; a war ax had cleaved her skull from behind as she fought to aid her husband.

McCabe turned as Gary came up. "Wringle must be around somewhere, Jim. Take a look over there, where he was building. A man usually defends first what he prizes."

Gary walked over to the burned structure, not caring whether he found Wringle or not; he had seen enough to prove that the Comanches had broken their treaty, that a new war had begun, and that a lot of men on both sides would die before this was settled again. He wondered if this would ever be settled, for the second treaty would mean less than the first, there would be more to remember, and more to forgive, and man, red and white, had a small tolerance for forgiveness.

He found Wringle, dead, vacant-eyed, the eyeballs rolled upward as though he were trying to inspect the crimson patch where his scalp-lock had been; Gary turned away and walked back to where Guthie McCabe waited.

"You going to put all this in your report, Jim?"

"I don't want to," Gary said. "See if you can find a couple of shovels. We'll bury them."

McCabe found one shovel, and a spade; he gave the shovel to Gary so his digging would be easier, and Gary looked curiously at him for a moment, but said nothing about this. They worked for three hours, barely pausing, and then they wrapped both bodies into a blanket and buried them together. At last the mound of earth was tamped and McCabe threw his spade aside.

"I'll find his ax and cut something for a marker."

"No," Gary said. "Take the horses and run them over the grave until it's trampled flat."

McCabe frowned, yet his eyes contained a speculative hope. "Jim, what are you thinking of?"

"Another Indian war," Gary said. "This isn't going in my report, Guthrie." He waved his hand. "Yeah, I know, the army and all that, but this is something I've got to do. Stone Calf's sons were only avenging their father, and that was my fault. You were right. I should have left Janice Tremain alone. As it turned out, we'd have picked her up anyway, without all this."

"No, I wasn't right," McCabe said softly. "Just thought I was right. A lot of things have changed, Jim. I lived in hell and I'm not the same man as before." He sat down on the mound and looked at him. "Jim, if nothing is done about this, nothing said, the Comanches will get bold and kill others. You want that on your conscience?"

"It'll be up to me to see that that doesn't happen. Guthrie, I'll be going back to Iron Hand with a lot of questions. I'll hold back his beef ration and dog him and worry him half to death over this, but I won't be able to prove anything. I'm going to put the fear into him so this won't happen again." He put his shovel aside and sat down beside McCabe. "This isn't easy for me. All my life I've lived as right as I could, done what's right, studied the rules and believed in them. But I've never done much good, except maybe this, what I'm doing now. There won't be any war. Peace is here and it's going to stay that way. Wringle and his wife bought and paid for it and I wouldn't sell them short."

Guthrie McCabe laughed softly. "For a minute there I thought your do-gooder morals were going to get the best of you, Jim."

"No, I've learned to bend them." He looked at McCabe. "You sure as hell didn't make much out of this, did you?"

McCabe threw back his head and laughed. "I've never come out any shorter in my life. But I'm not crying about it, Jim. Damned funny, that. Somehow I no longer feel that I have to apologize for my intentions." He tapped Gary on

113

the arm. "You figure you can look the colonel in the eye and lie to him? You've never done it before."

"I'll do it. Lying isn't so bad, or so hard, once you make up your mind to it."

"You're learning," McCabe said, and got up. "We going to stay here?"

"No. I guess we're finished."

They threw the tools into the nearby rubble, then mounted and turned out, cutting toward the column's calculated position. After a time, Gary said. "Well, one thing, the Miles woman will have built up a big yearning for you, Guthrie."

"Yeah, but I've lost mine for her. The goddamned house was full of drafts anyway, and the roof leaked like a sieve when it rained." He shot Gary a wry glance. "Tascosa will look good to me now. Real good."

"One thing bothers me," Gary said frankly. "I like you, McCabe, but I can't make up my mind whether it's because you're less of a bastard than when we started, or if I'm more of one."

They rested for two hours at midday when the heat was highest, then pushed on slowly, calculating time and speed to meet the column and yet conserve their animals. Because of this, Gary arrived three hours late, well after dark, guided the last few miles by the squad fires.

A trooper took their horses and both men went to Lieutenant Shea's fire at the head of the camp. He was sitting on a folding canvas stool, filling in his daily report; he rose quickly when Gary and McCabe stepped into the firelight. Both men were tired, dirty, and not inclined to talk, yet this did not stop Shea.

"Was everything all right at Sand Creek, sir?"

"Everything was fine."

"The Wringles were all right?"

Gary frowned. "Mr. Shea, the Wringles were not there. Obviously they thought better of it and returned to Fort Elliot. Now where's the coffee? We haven't had a meal or a decent sit down since leaving you."

"Sergeant Davis has been holding some food, sir. Third fire over."

"Thank you," Gary said and walked over with McCabe.

"Jim," McCabe said softly, "we forgot to trample the grave."

"I know it, but don't think I'm going back to do it." Davis started to get up as they approached, but Gary waved him back. "What is it, Sergeant? Beef and beans?"

"Yes, sir. I saved a pot, figuring you'd come in before midnight." He handed a plate to each of them and they hunkered

114

down to eat. Davis waited a moment, then said, "Mr. McCabe, you speak Comanche. I wish you'd talk to the prisoners. They're giving us a devil of a time, sir. All the time trying to escape and go back."

"It's up to Gary," McCabe said. "I'm a civilian."

"We'll go over after we eat," Gary said and wiped his plate clean before accepting a second helping. After he finished his coffee, he patted his pockets for a smoke, but found none. Sergeant Davis offered them his own brand, and after taking a light, they passed through the camp to the outskirts where the white returnees were being held under strong guard.

"Seems a shame that they have to be prisoners now that they're rescued," Gary said. He pointed to a woman in her early twenties. "Ask her her name, McCabe."

He did, then translated. "Shy Deer, or so she says. I think she speaks English."

"Do you speak English?" Gary asked.

"Yes," she said. "I was eight when the Comanches took me." Three small children stood half-hidden behind her; they stared at the two men with walnut-colored eyes. "Where do you take us?"

"To the fort," Gary said. "Your family is there."

She shook her head. "My family is dead. I remember."

McCabe glanced at Gary. "What are you going to do about that, Jim? You take her from one place where she had a home and turn her loose at Fort Elliot?"

"Do I have a choice?" He drew on his cigar. "Tell all of them to behave themselves. I can only take them to their rightful families who wait at Fort Elliot."

McCabe told them and they moaned and wailed and some of the young men struggled against the ropes that bound them. Gary turned away and started back to Shea's camp; McCabe walked beside him.

"Who's going to sort through these people when we get to Elliot, Jim? Or do you take them in with ropes around their necks and put them on the block like cattle?"

"Colonel Frazer will have to take that responsibility."

"If they never got there——"

Gary cut him off sharply. "Then another officer would round them up! Guthrie, when I had to kill that man, you told me why you hung back and watched the whole thing through your field glasses. This is the same thing. It's do it now and do it as clean as you can, then try to forget what you've done."

"Well, you've toughened up some," McCabe said. "But are you tough enough to forget it?"

"I don't know," Gary said. "I wish I did know."

The return march to Fort Elliot was a trial to Jim Gary, because he was in command, yet every man in the column suffered. The white captives slowed them down by every means, singing and chanting continually to wear on the troopers' nerves and make the horses skittish, and never letting up at night so anyone could sleep. The young men staged mock riots among themselves, butting heads and kicking, forcing the guard to be doubled, and keeping troopers on their feet when they should have been in their blankets.

Gary was vastly relieved to see Fort Elliot in the distance, and more relieved when the officer-of-the-day and a five-man detail rode out to meet him.

"You're late, Gary," the officer said, drawing up. "But that's no matter. The colonel wants you to report to him. Take your command into the post. We'll take charge of the rescued group." He studied them, a frown building on his forehead. "Why are they bound and under guard?"

"To keep them from running away," Gary said. "Unless you want them to scatter, better keep them under strong guard."

"We'll attend to it," the officer said. "Report to Colonel Frazer immediately, Gary."

"Oh, sure," Gary said, and rode on.

There was the business of dismissing his men, and seeing that the animals were tended. Afterward he and McCabe walked to headquarters and found Frazer impatiently pacing up and down his office.

"When I request an officer's presence, I mean before he tends to his private toilet," Frazer said. "Sit down. McCabe, you can wait outside."

"This is good enough," McCabe said and took a chair. Frazer did not like this, but decided not to press the matter.

"Report, Lieutenant Gary."

"Forty-seven adult whites recovered, sir, male and female. About nineteen children, mixed blood."

"By God, you carried it off!" Frazer was jubilant.

"We sure did," McCabe said dryly. "You'll be a big-assed hero with the Washington politicians, Colonel."

"McCabe, I'll thank you to keep your mouth shut," Frazer said. He raised his voice. "Orderly! Bring in the pay voucher!" A moment later a private brought in the book and Frazer signed a sheet, then tore it out. "Take this to the paymaster and get off the post, McCabe. I told you once that I'd take great pleasure in throwing you off, and now I'm doing it. If you're not gone by evening, I'll have the officer-of-the-day eject you bodily."

McCabe was studying the voucher; when he looked at Fra-

116

zer he did so with anger in his eyes. "What the hell is this? Three weeks pay."

"You'll, find that correct, sir," Frazer said. "And quite legal. You don't think the army is going to pay you for time spent under some squaw's blanket, do you?" He laughed heartily. "You're bested, McCabe. Taken at your own game. Now clear out of this office."

"Sure," McCabe said flatly. "See you outside, Jim." He let the door slam behind him and Frazer went behind his desk, a smile wreathing his face.

"You don't know how much pleasure that gives me, Gary. And I take pleasure in telling you that you've done a good job. Within months now you'll hear word on your promotion."

"Yes, sir." Gary locked his teeth together to keep from telling Frazer what to do with the promotion. Get out, that was his thought; get out before he opened his mouth and blew his military career sky high. "What will the disposition be of the returnees, sir?"

"Not your concern," Frazer said. "They wanted their kin back and now they've got them. It'll straighten itself out. By George, the army can't do everything for them." He smiled in a fatherly fashion at Gary. "You've had rough duty, my boy. Consider yourself relieved for the next five days. Draw your pay and go into Tascosa. Have a good time."

"Yes, sir. That sounds like excellent advice. Will that be all, sir?"

"Yes, you're dismissed—Captain." He winked when he said it and forever stained the rank in Gary's mind; he felt as though he had been handed a dozen filthy post cards while in church; in his mind there was an almost reverence for military service, a religious adherence to his duty, but it would never be that way again.

He stepped outside and found McCabe standing in the shade of the porch. Gary said, "I'm footloose for the next five days. Let's ride."

"I'd kind of like to see that Donovan girl first," McCabe said. "You feel like going out to the camp by the creek?"

"Sure," Gary said. "I've got to face them sometime."

21

The civilan camp was in turmoil when Gary and McCabe arrived, for the white prisoners were being pawed over and argued over, and given out to the people foolish enough to claim them. The group that Gary and McCabe had taken to Sand Creek stayed near their wagons, yet there was a carnival atmosphere in the camp while mothers were separated from their half-Indian children; the relatives did not want them at all, just their own, while the captives wanted none of their relatives.

The army was there, trying to establish order, but there is little order in emotion, and the camp was a boil of it, ready for lancing, and Jim Gary did not want to see the operation, being able to guess at the poison that would be released.

McCabe left him and went on to the Donovan wagon while Gary observed the slave-block tactics and let the sounds of crying and pleading soak into him; he seemed to desire punishment for his part in this, and to see it was punishment enough, for this was something he would carry in his mind for the rest of his life.

The Donovan wagon was parked near the creek, but the sounds still carried to it. Jane gave McCabe some coffee, examined the scar on his hand to make certain it had healed properly, then sat down on the dropped wagon tongue.

"I wonder how many of this bunch they'll hang."

"Jim's thinking that, you can bet on it."

"Where is he? Why didn't he come with you?"

McCabe shrugged. "I guess he's got his reasons. I only came to say good-by. Jim and I are going into Tascosa for a few days. Probably you'll be gone when he comes back."

"You sound like you're making a speech for him, Guthrie."

"Maybe I am without knowing it," he said. "Jane, right now he needs someone who understands without a lot of talk, but I don't think he'll come to you. You can see why not, can't you?"

"Yes, but he tried to do right."

McCabe shook his head. "That isn't good enough for men like Jim Gary." He smiled and handed his half-empty cup to her. "Too bad you're not going to stay, Jane. You'd be good for him."

"Would I? I've been asking myself that."

"The Tremain woman, is she still on the post? He'll want to know."

"She left with her uncle. California, I think. He's retiring after this term of office. Tell Jim; it's a drop of good news among an ocean of bad."

"I'll tell him."

He started to turn away but she took his arm and held him back. "I have to know, Guthrie. Was he in love with her?"

This made him laugh. "No. He was full of gallantry but he wasn't in love. That's something that Jim wouldn't pass out to the first pretty woman that came along."

"Thank you. That makes it easier."

He left her then and walked rapidly across the camp to the crowd gathered around the army and their charges. Gary saw him coming and came to meet him.

"I'm sick enough," Gary said. "Let's go." He sided McCabe and they re-entered the post. In the stable, saddling their horses, Gary came out with it. "Guthrie, I hope you said my good-bys for me."

"No, I didn't. You damn fool, you don't ever want to say good-by to a girl like that." He tightened the cinch, then stepped into the saddle. "She'll be here when you get back. I've got a feeling." ·

"I wish I had it." He mounted his horse. "Let's go see the paymaster."

The office was in one wing of the guardhouse near the main gate, and Gary drew his pay while McCabe settled for his paltry amount. The guard let them pass through and they turned to the Tascosa road, facing a full twenty-hour ride.

They camped early and were in their blankets before a full darkness settled, and before dawn they were moving on. Gary veered off the road and headed toward Anson Miles's place. This brought a sharp look from McCabe.

"I don't have to go there, Jim."

"A man always ought to look at a thing he's wanted badly after he's decided he doesn't want it," Gary said. "It sort of removes all doubt."

"All right," McCabe said. "Have it your own way."

The multi-roomed mansion at last began to loom before them, larger and larger as they closed the distance. Passing into the front yard, both men sat their horses and waited for Miles's dog to come yap-snapping out of the barn, but he remained hidden. Gary rode on up to the porch, leaned from the saddle and knocked on the post, but no one came out. Both men then rode around the place and saw that all the shutters were nailed closed.

"What the hell goes on here?" McCabe asked.

"Maybe there's an answer in town," Gary said and turned in that direction.

They approached it in darkness, tied up before the saloon and went inside. The hour was late and only a few men stood at the bar. In a corner a dull poker game plodded along with bored players and low stakes.

"McCabe!" the bartender said, placing a bottle on the bar. "When did you get back?"

"Just now," McCabe said. He looked around the room once, then let his traveling glance stop at a corner table. A nudge drew Gary's attention and he also looked. Anson Miles had his bottle, glass, and his thoughts; he acted as though he never cared to look up again.

"Let's go have a talk with him," McCabe suggested, taking bottle and glasses with him. They sat down at Miles's table and it seemed that he would never glance at them.

He spoke without raising his eyes. "Hear you come in, Guthrie. How you been, Lieutenant?"

"Tolerable," Gary said. "And you?"

"The same. I'm going to get drunk. You want to stay and see it?"

"What you want to do that for?" McCabe asked. "I never knew you to suck the bottle, Anson."

"The world looks better when I'm drunk," Miles said. Then he looked at McCabe. "You left her alone too long, Guthrie. Now we've both lost her."

"What the hell you talking about?"

"My little wife, that's who I'm talking about." He laughed. "I wanted a new windmill put up. A salesman came out from Kansas City. She rolled her eyes and he smiled with them pretty white teeth he had, and the next day she up and ran off with him. That's why I'm getting drunk." He studied McCabe for a moment, then smiled. "Why don't you get drunk too?"

"No reason."

"You got a reason," Miles said.

"Then tell it to me."

"You ain't sheriff no more. Nope, they threw you out for going away like you did. Guthrie, folks will stand for just so much you know, and you always was one for bending a thing out of shape."

Jim Gary spoke up. "All this talk isn't getting us anywhere. What we need is another bottle, one apiece. Hey, bartender."

"This boy's got a head on him," Miles said. "How come I never saw that before?"

"You were sober," Guthrie McCabe said.

120

The bottle was produced and each man filled his glass. McCabe offered the toast, for they were gentlemen with a common intent. "Here's to all the beauty in the world. May a strong wind come up and blow the dust off it."

"Amen," Miles said. Their glasses were immediately emptied.

McCabe said, "Hey, Jim, you forgot to send money to your sisters. Better put some of that in another pocket."

Gary shook his head. "I've already figured out how many bottles it'll buy."

"Now you've grown selfish," McCabe said. "A toast, to youthful ideals destroyed."

The bottles were upped, the glasses upped; three men sighed and wiped tears from their eyes. Miles's voice was getting thick because he had a head start on them, but McCabe and Gary quickly caught up with him.

Closing time was midnight on week nights, and the bartender turned out the back lamps before approaching their table. They reeled in their chairs, sang songs together, laughed over nothing, and cried for their own private reasons. The bartender was disgusted with them; he secretly hated drunks, having taken the Keely Cure once himself, and their crying angered him. He saw the tears and nothing more, and he spoke roughly to them.

"Time to get out! Come on, let's go!"

They paid no attention to him and when he tried to take Gary's arm, the young man knocked him down. The bartender was more surprised than hurt, and when he got up, he went out and down the street after the sheriff.

Lon Caswell had been a deputy under McCabe and he could not help but recall all those times he had bent his will to McCabe's. He handled Miles gently, carrying him off to jail, then came back for Lieutenant Gary. McCabe was saved to the last, slapped around a little and handled roughly, but he was too drunk to care.

They shared the same cell, and after locking the door, Caswell sat in his office, dozing until dawn. A buggy rattling down the street woke him and he got up to see who it was. Then he saw that it was an army ambulance driven by a burly sergeant. A young woman shared the seat beside him and the rig stopped in front of the jail.

Jane Donovan got down with the sergeant's help and came across the walk.

"Are you the sheriff?"

"Yes'm."

"Then you're the one I want to see," she said, stepping into his office. "It occurs to me that you might have a gentle-

man here who had too much to drink. I've come to get him."
Caswell smiled. "I expect you mean Lieutenant Gary. Yes'm,
he's sleeping it off now."

"Is there a fine?"

"No," Caswell said. "They had quite a crying jag on last
night, Miss—"

"Donovan," she said. "Will it be all right to take Lieutenant
Gary back to the post now?"

"Sure, it just saves me county expense of feeding him."
Caswell went to the cell block to get Gary and Sergeant Davis
came inside to help him into the back of the ambulance. Gary
could hardly walk and he did not open his eyes; rather he
held them tightly shut as though he was afraid to open them.
Caswell came to stand in the doorway and Jane Donovan
and the sergeant climbed into the rig.

They U-turned in the street and left Tascosa without delay.
Jane kept her hands clasped tightly together in her lap for
a mile or so, then she said, "Perhaps I should have waited
and let him come back by himself, Sergeant. But I had my
fears that he wouldn't come back."

"Lieutenant Gary's not one to give a thing up," Davis said.
"He's army, ma'am."

"Yes," she said. Then she looked at him, her eyes shining
with seriousness, dedication. "We'll have to look after him
for awhile, Sergeant. You, when he's on duty, and me, when
he's off. We can't fail him. You understand?"

"Yes'm." Then he put his gloved hand on hers; the rough
planes of his cheeks broke into a smile. "Lieutenant Gary's
just too good a man to lose. And we sure won't lose him,
ma'am. Don't you worry about it."

"My, I forgot about Guthrie McCabe! Turn about, Sergeant. Perhaps the sheriff will——"

"No, no," Davis said, shaking his head. "Mr. McCabe will
sober up soon enough, then he and the sheriff will play a
little game to see who gets the badge." He laughed. "Ma'am,
there's nothing wrong with McCabe, except maybe a headache. He never asks a man for a favor." Davis laughed. "I've
known the man since I was transferred here. If someone steals
his place, he just roots another one." Davis clucked to the
team. "I give him sixty days, or until the Colonel is gone.
Then he'll come riding out to the fort with a smile and a
badge on his vest and money jingling in his pockets. The
McCabes in this world are hard to put down, ma'am. Be glad
of it."

"Yes," she said softly. "Now, I think I am glad."

FROM THE PRODUCER OF
THE KENT FAMILY CHRONICLES
WAGONS WEST—VOLUME II

NEBRASKA
by Dana Fuller Ross

Here is a special preview
of the exciting opening pages of the
second book in this sweeping saga of the
men and women whose lives were
caught up in America's westward drive.

1

Heavy clouds, thick and black, ominous in their intensity, blew eastward from the Rocky Mountains across the Great Plains wilderness, obscuring the moon and stars. The night air had been cool, but the ground was still warm from the early autumn sun that had shone down on Missouri the previous day, so a white mist, as impenetrable as a bale of cotton, rose from the broad waters of the great Missouri River, bathing the whole area in a blanket of swirling mists.

High on the bluffs of the eastern bank of the river, a short distance from the frontier village of Independence, stood the symbols of the future. Wagon after wagon arranged in a circle. Flexible wooden hoops were looped upward over their sides and covered with thick canvas to protect the inhabitants from the elements. There were scores of wagons, hundreds of men, women and children in the caravan, all of them asleep. They were the first pioneers who would blaze a path to the Pacific Ocean and, in the decades to come, would be followed by thousands of others making their way to the Oregon Territory and California.

Some had already traveled all the way from

the Eastern seaboard, to be joined by others along the way in a daring venture unique in the annals of the history of the young United States. Only optimists, only Americans, would have dreamed such dreams of the future or dared to make such a long trek into the unknown.

Inside the circle, the horses and oxen were asleep, too, as were the dogs. None stirred.

There seemed to be nothing to fear. Independence was a sturdy little community of ranch owners and farmers—people who took the law into their own hands when need be because no other law existed at this remote outpost. Bloodshed was not unknown, but violence occurred infrequently.

No one in the wagon train heard the two boats being rowed across the Missouri from the west bank with muffled oars. No one saw the little craft hauled ashore, beached and made secure. Certainly no one in the train knew that six armed men, frontier drifters who preyed on fur trappers or isolated farm owners, were finding the train a target too tempting to be left in peace. There were animals to steal, valuables to snatch—prizes for desperadoes who placed small value on human life.

The six men crept up the hill, pistols and knives in their hands. A shepherd dog stretched outside one of the wagons awakened and raised its pointed ears. The bandits crept closer, struggling quietly as they made their way up the palisade.

One member of the wagon train stirred. Tall and lean, dressed in the buckskins, he was sound asleep one moment, completely awake and alert the next. He reached for his long rifle automatically and rose to his feet with effortless grace, in a single move.

A glance told him the mist was too thick for him to see, so he listened intently, his head cocked to one side. Then a faint, grim smile appeared on his face. Moving silently, with the experience of one who had spent years as a hunter, trapper and guide in the Rockies, he went quickly to several key wagons.

In almost no time he was joined by a motley group of men, carrying rifles. The trio followed the man in buckskins to the lip of the bluff. No one could see much more than a few feet ahead—certainly no one in the group could hear anything untoward. Within a few seconds they were joined by an Indian brave, also clad in buckskins—a warrior who almost casually notched an arrow in his bow. Like the man in buckskins, he had no need to see the approaching menace.

The marauders came still closer. They were no more than fifty feet from the top of the bluff. A broad smile appeared on the face of the man in buckskins. There was no doubt that he thoroughly enjoyed the challenge of danger. He didn't need to speak; his companions had traveled far with him, and knew what was expected of them.

Now the robbers were no more than five

yards from the lip of the palisade, almost within reach of their goal. The man in buckskins nodded, almost laconically, and four rifles spoke simultaneously, the weapons deliberately fired over the heads of the approaching foe.

The startled bandits paused, then turned and fled down the steep slope, sliding and stumbling, falling and scrambling as they raced to the safety of their waiting boat.

Now it was the Indian's turn. He sent arrow after arrow toward the retreating enemies. The bandits saw the arrows dropping among them and increased their wild pace as they dragged their boat into the water and rowed off to safety.

The man in buckskins listened, heard the fading sound of oars, and nodded. His companions turned and strolled back to their wagons for another hour of sleep. He rolled himself in his blanket. The Indian followed his example. Within a few minutes they had drifted back to sleep.

The ears of the shepherd dog drooped again, and the mist was still thick. The men, women and children of the train were deep in slumber. Even those who had awakened briefly had mistaken the firearms volley for a crack of thunder.

The wagon train was secure.

As always Cathy van Ayl looked lovely as she emerged from her wagon, and as always she seemed unaware of her beauty. She paused on the back step to tuck some stray strands of her long, blonde hair under her sunbonnet, then tightened the sash of her dimity dress. She looked like a young girl in her teens rather than a widow of twenty-three, but that innocence wasn't accidental. Her elderly husband, Otto, a miserly farmer from Long Island who had died in a raid on the wagon train had never been affectionate toward her.

Cathy finished primping just as Whip Holt, the hired guide and wagonmaster of the Oregon-bound caravan, came into view. Tall and sinewy in his buckskins, he was armed, as usual, with a brace of pistols and the long bullwhip, wrapped about his middle, that gave him his name. His skin was leathery after a lifetime of exposure to the outdoors, and his eyes were hard. Then he saw Cathy, and when he grinned at her he suddenly looked younger than twenty-nine.

She smiled at him in return, her heart skipping a beat. When her husband was alive she'd had to conceal her interest in Whip, but all that had changed. Now she had no reason beyond her own sense of discretion to hide the way she felt.

Certainly Whip made no secret of his own feelings. "Morning, ma'am," he called, sauntering toward her.

"You're wearing a new buckskin shirt and trousers, I see," she said politely.

He was startled that she noticed what he was wearing. "Well, you know how it is. I get restless just sitting around Independence while we put in supplies and wait for the new folks joining us to show up. So one day I took me hunting." He cleared his throat awkwardly. "You look mighty nice, all dressed up for a day in the city."

Cathy couldn't help laughing. Certainly no one else in 1837 would dream of referring to the frontier town of Independence, Missouri, as a "city." The last outpost of civilization east of the Great Plains, it was visited by trappers, hunters and traders bringing their furs from the Rocky Mountains to the East. Now, with other wagon trains scheduled to follow Whip's caravan across the wilderness to the fertile Oregon country, Independence promised to develop into a major supply center.

"I told my sister I'd buy some things in town for her and bring them along tonight."

Only a few days earlier Cathy's older sister, Claudia, had been married to Sam Brentwood, the former leader of the wagon train. The couple would remain in Independence to establish a supply depot, sponsored by Sam's mentors, former President of the United States Andrew Jackson, and John Jacob Astor, a fur baron, leader of a group of wealthy businessmen who were encouraging the American settlement of the Oregon territory.

"Claudia and Sam asked me to supper tonight, too," Whip said, and shifted in embarrassment. "I—I wasn't so sure I wanted to go, seeing as how I don't sit me down at a table indoors very often. But if you're going, ma'am, I'll be happy to escort you."

"I'd like that," Cathy said. She smiled again before turning away, then added, "I'm not really dressed up, you know. All I own are a few dresses like this, except for the old woolen things I wear on the trail."

"Could you use a doeskin dress, ma'am?"

"I'd love it, Whip." Cathy hesitated. "But I wouldn't want you to think I was hinting."

"No matter. Stalking Horse," he said, referring to his close friend, a Cherokee scout, "has been pestering me to try our hands at hunting again, so I reckon I'll have some skins for you by the time we push off."

Cathy thanked him, discomfited by his generousity, then left the circle of wagons. Directly ahead, beyond the bend in the Missouri River, stood the limitless wilderness that stretched across the Great Plains, the Rocky Mountains and, on the far side of the Continental Divide, yet another chain of mountains which the wagon train would have to cross before reaching Oregon.

Otto van Ayl had given his wife no choice and had been determined to go to Oregon. But the widowed Cathy had an alternative and was free to make up her own mind. Claudia and Sam had offered her a home with them, right here in Independence. And she wouldn't be dependent on their charity, either. Her wagon was as solid as any made in

New England, where they had originated in the days prior to the War of Independence. The four horses which pulled it were strong, surefooted and healthy. She could get a substantial sum for the wagon and team if she decided to stay behind when the train moved out. In addition, Otto had left her the fortune he had saved in a lifetime of miserly living, two thousand dollars in gold. When they started on the journey; Otto had concealed the money beneath a false floor in the wagon, but after his death, at Claudia and Sam's insistence, she had moved it for safekeeping to the enormous special wagon where the caravan's medicines, extra weapons and emergency rations were stored.

So Cathy was wealthy, at least by the standards of the emigrants who were heading out to Oregon. Certainly she could pay for her keep if she decided to stay with her sister and new brother-in-law. Fortunately she wouldn't have to make up her mind for a few days; there were influences pulling her in both directions.

Because of Whip she wanted to go on. But she was a grown woman, not a romantic adolescent, and she couldn't allow her interest in him to become too great a factor. It was true, however, that she believed in finishing what she started, and if any of the stories she had heard about Oregon were true, it was heaven on earth.

Tugging her in the opposite direction was the knowledge that powerful forces were at work trying to prevent the American settlers from reaching their destination. The ownership of the Oregon country was in dispute, with both the United States and Great Britain claiming it. A British agent, Henry St. Clair, had already made several violent attempts to halt the train, even inspiring a vicious attack on the caravan by Army deserters. Although that last attempt had failed, several members of the company had been killed. And the pioneers would not have been comforted, had they known the thoughts that were still going through St. Clair's head. By God, he promised himself, they're not going to beat me! Hell or high water, I'm going to stop that damn wagon train!

But the British attempt to sabotage the train wasn't the only one. Imperial Russia wanted to stop them from reaching Oregon, too. Russians had been the first to settle in Oregon. Although international pressures had forced the czar seemingly to abandon his claim, the government in St. Petersburg was actually doing no such thing. Cathy was one of the few members of the caravan who knew that attempts had been made by the *Cheka*, the czar's secret police, to blackmail a lovely, frontier-wise girl named Tonie Mell into working for them. Tonie's parents, whom she hadn't seen since early childhood, were still in Russia. She had been told they wouldn't be allowed to join her unless she committed acts of sabotage against the train. Thanks to her own courage and the help of

Sam and Whip, she had outsmarted them.
But it was fair to assume that the Russians
would try again.

In addition, there were terrifying rumors
among the settlers about the hostile Indian
tribes in the wilderness ahead. There were
some pessimists who predicted that every last
man, woman and child in the train would be
murdered. But Cathy refused to believe such
rubbish. No matter how great the menace of
Indians might become, she had unbounded
faith in Whip Holt's abilities. She had seen
him in action, and she was confident he
would lead the band of settlers, already four
hundred strong and growing every day, to
their Oregon destination in safety. She was
convinced that no Indians could prevent
Whip from reaching his goal—for that matter, neither could the British and Russians.

Tonight, perhaps, she would discuss the decision with her sister; it might clarify her own
thinking.

The wagon train had made camp outside
Independence, where the horses and oxen
could graze, and Cathy headed toward the
town. She passed log cabins and houses of
whitewashed clapboard. Until the past year,
Independence had been little more than a
village. But now it boasted two general
stores, a stable, and, on its main street, two
brothels and at least a dozen taverns and sa-
loons. When Sam and Claudia finished making changes in the ranch, their property

would become the principal supply depot for later wagon trains.

The depot would sell both horses and oxen, as well as spare wheels, axles and yokes. Thanks to Claudia's experience on the long march from New York to Missouri, she planned to put in a full supply of such provisions as bacon, flour, beans and sugar—the staples that every immigrant family needed on the trek across the continent. Thanks to the generosity of Astor and his associates, as well as the official encouragement of President Martin Van Buren, Sam would have enough funds to put in a stock of firearms, gunpowder and ammunition, too.

The morning sun was warm, almost hot, the breeze was gentle and it seemed more like summer than the beginning of autumn. It was small wonder that Whip was eager to start the march across the plains as soon as possible. Cathy knew from her own experience in the past six months that the caravan could travel ten to twelve miles per day in good weather, but that progress was slowed to a crawl when it rained. When the rains were very heavy it sometimes became necessary to call a complete halt.

Pondering her decision, paying scant attention to her immediate surroundings, Cathy was suddenly aroused from her reverie by the sound of a man's harsh, deep voice.

"That there one is the prettiest I've seen since we got to this town. I claim her!"

"Like hell you do," another man, replied. "Maybe we'll draw lots for her, all of us, or maybe we'll leave the choice up to her. We got to be fair about this."

The startled Cathy saw eight or nine men who had just emerged from a tavern directly ahead. In spite of the early hour, they had been drinking heavily. Some of them were dressed in shabby linsey-woolsey and others in worn, greasy buckskins. They had not shaved for days and their hair was dirty and unkempt. All were armed with skinning knives, as well as either pistols or rifles.

These were the men Whip and Sam contemptuously referred to as "frontier scum," opportunists who earned a precarious living. Sometimes they bought furs from trappers down on their luck and sold them to traders. Sometimes they did odd jobs for local homesteaders. They were as unsavory as they were unreliable, and Cathy blamed herself for failing to see them in time to avoid them.

But she had little time for regrets. The group had spread across the road, blocking her path, and she was afraid, judging by their leers, that they would maul her if she tried to crowd past them. But she might be in even worse trouble if she turned and tried to flee; certainly that would encourage them in their game. There were no other pedestrians, no riders in sight, so it would be useless to call for help.

The best way to handle the situation, she decided, would be to keep moving forward, remaining calm, and ignoring the brutes. She was tempted to pick up her flounced skirt and run, but instead she continued to walk at the same, even pace, her head high.

One of her tormentors muttered something, and the group quickly surrounded the girl. The man with the rasping voice, appointing himself the spokesman, grinned at her. "You look like you need some lovin'," he said, "so take your pick."

"Let me pass, please." Cathy knew no escape was possible, but made an effort to speak calmly.

"Don't put on no airs with us, girlie," another declared. "You women up the road charge enough, so it's high time you give us somethin' free."

The stunned Cathy suddenly realized they had mistaken her for a girl from one of the brothels. Certainly they were in no mood—perhaps in no condition—to heed her denials. She was in real danger and she didn't know how to escape.

Follow the lives of Whip and Cathy, Claudia and Sam, and all those people who continue the hazardous journey from Independence to Nebraska. Their ultimate destination—Oregon. Read the complete book, to be available July 1, wherever Bantam Books are sold.

"REACH FOR THE SKY!"

and you still won't find more excitement or more thrills than you get in Bantam's slam-bang, action-packed westerns! Here's a roundup of fast-reading stories by some of America's greatest western writers: